MARRIED CHRISTMAS, HAPPY HOLIDAYS

CLAIRE CAIN

Cover design by Jess Mastorakos - Jess@jessmastorakos.com

EBOOK ISBN: 978-1-954005-73-0

PRINT ISBN: 978-1-954005-74-7

To anyone who adopts animals—you're the tops. Merry Christmas and Happy Holidays, friends.

CHAPTER ONE

Janie

THEN

I didn't expect Elvis to bear witness when I'm reunited with my childhood best friend-slash-lifelong crush who's made an extreme sport of ghosting me.

My heart isn't prepared to see Colin Vicente after so long. Is it his military uniform and that regal bearing he's always had that makes me want to climb him, and also slap him? Or is it the cruel reality that I've loved him since I knew what crushes and butterflies were, and it feels like maybe I haven't effectively purged those feelings like I thought I had?

Not even stripping the house to the studs would clear those out.

Nor am I mentally prepared to see him, and I'll be having words with the bride on the matter at some point after her super special Christmastime in Vegas nuptials. He isn't supposed to be here, period.

The light sweat breaking out across my skin and tumbling stomach at the simple sight of him is more than he deserves. More than a mature, self-possessed woman celebrating her friends should feel for a man who has had virtually zero part in her life recently.

My heart has given far too much time to Colin Vicente, and considering I haven't seen him since he left for West Point years ago, the whole heart-flipping business is utter nonsense. Out of sight, out of mind, and all that should be how this goes. Or in this case, heart.

And now, here he is shouldering his way back into sight again.

And what a sight indeed.

He left our hometown for the Academy at eighteen and he was handsome then, but still a teen.

Now, his dark hair is close-cropped, though not as severely as it had been years ago. He's got the steady gaze and those creases in his cheeks making his bone structure look even more harshly beautiful. His eyes are that same dark brown, a rich well of color I loved to look at because they changed with whatever shirt color he wore. Now, in his dark olive-green uniform, they'd have hints of gold and green, too.

Not that I'm looking.

Not that I care.

Why should I, when in all the years he's been away, I haven't heard from him once? I wanted to. Wished to. Begged the stars hanging over both our heads to change something. But even when my heart was tender and hopeful, I eventually squashed all of that noise under my foot.

It just ended up being more like stepping in old gum. The sticky residue changed the way it felt to walk around.

"Well, the major's looking fearsome," Danica, my fellow bridesmaid, whispers in my ear, her eyes assessing every centimeter of my face.

"Shh! You're not supposed to talk." I jab an elbow into her side, and a muffled grunt gives me satisfaction.

Andrea, maid of honor at-large, glares over her shoulder, then whips her head back to watch as the Velvet Elvis come to life asks the couple in front of our devoted line to exchange rings. I pin my gaze to them, refusing to let my eyes wander back to the man in question.

He showed up late, slipped into place, and when Charlie, the groom, caught sight of him, he paused the ceremony and went to give Colin a huge, back-slapping hug.

Honestly, it was adorable. For as terrible a friend as he's been to me, Colin's evidently a real hero for showing up. He also looks like an actual hero because he's wearing that uniform, and despite my best efforts, I find a man in uniform endlessly attractive.

Does it stem from the first time I saw a photo of *him* in uniform from his college graduation?

No.

Obviously.

Why would I even think that?

"I now pronounce you husband and wife. You may kiss the bride!"

A cheer rises around us, clapping, whistling, as Charlie dips Lindy low and kisses her. Her golden veil nearly falls, but thanks to an assist from Andrea, who holds the yards of tulle up so it doesn't catch on Lindy's sparkling, five-inch stiletto heels, it all stays put.

I clap, emotion swelling in my chest as I watch my friends right themselves and turn to face the small crowd in the chapel. The applause grows louder when their recessional plays and they literally rock out, hands and arms flailing, back down the aisle.

That's when I realize it—right as Andrea walks up and takes the best man's arm, then Danica takes the next groomsman's arm, and then, *gulp*, it's my turn. There was no one in the procession for me at rehearsals. Lindy never said a thing, and somehow, Charlie didn't either.

Rude.

I walk to the center of the aisle and look up in time to meet his eyes, as devastatingly deep brown as they ever were, layered today with flecks of gold and green. I hate how well I know those eyes, even now.

"Hey, CP."

And just like that, we're moving down the aisle, despite his using my nickname from another life lighting a little fuse in my belly because honestly, how dare he? Does he really think we can pick up from where we left off? Is he conveniently forgetting he's been radio silent for a decade now?

On autopilot, I've slipped my arm in his and we're walking abreast, but our gazes are locked, and all the frustration and hurt is melting into something messy and urgent. *How dare you show up here looking so handsome and like everything's fine? Where have you been? Why are you here?* It's all churning, reaching, bubbling up and threatening to overflow—

"You guys, that was so fun, but now, we party!!!" Charlie and Lindy are still dancing and kissing, then swirling around to hug everyone.

Before I can make sense of anything happening in my head or body, Charlie rips Colin from me and hauls him into a bear hug.

I turn to find Lindy, eyes sparkling with tears as she yanks me into an embrace and holds me there.

"Please don't hate me. I was worried if I told you he was coming, you wouldn't, and I needed you here." She's dabbing at her cat-eye-lined lids, and I shake my head, instantly working to dispel the tears.

"Don't worry about a thing, okay? We'll catch up like old times and it'll be great." I grin as wide as I can without straining something. *Old times* will never happen again because I've boxed up the version of me who believed in that kind of closeness. A girl can only stand to be completely ditched by her best friend once. *Thanks, Major Vicente.* I wouldn't have missed tonight even if I had known he'd be here, but I would've been mentally armed against it. But that isn't the point tonight, so I add, "The ceremony was perfect."

"Right?" She beams.

Before long, we're shuttled into a limo and off to the hotel where we're all staying for the reception. Charlie and Lindy have friends from all over the world, so they decided on a destination wedding. Lindy's abiding love for Elvis informed the chapel choice and much of the décor, along with her golden wedding dress that is so sparkly it's likely visible in space if she steps outside for long.

Is that the Bellagio? The Vegas Sphere?

Nah, that's Lindy Portofino's wedding dress.

Colin is wedged between Charlie's best man and the other groomsman. They're gesticulating so wildly, I'm surprised Colin hasn't caught an elbow to the face yet, but I might not hate the sight of that.

Fine. I would feel bad. Especially if he were actually hurt.

Maybe.

His eyes slide to mine, and his stoic expression comes into focus. He is almost brutally handsome. He was always cute in a swoony, heart-aching kind of way, but his chiseled jaw and the mystery he's wrapped in gives him something frustratingly alluring.

A cork pops, and champagne flows into glasses Charlie hands off to each person in the vehicle. With Colin's eyes still burning a hole into mine, I gulp down half a glass before breaking the contact.

When my gaze flicks back to his, I see him taking a long drink from his own flute. The column of his throat moves, and his stupidly masculine Adam's apple bobs with his swallow.

I should not be finding this attractive, but there's heat at my cheeks and swirling around in my belly. He always had this effect on me. Why couldn't the years have changed that? Thankfully, Charlie and Lindy are leading the party in a round of car karaoke, and it's time to sing "Love Shack," so like a good little bridesmaid, I do.

My attention stays firmly off of Colin Vicente. I'll probably have to talk to him tonight, but another glass of champagne or two down the hatch should help.

By the time we reach the hotel, we've all imbibed more bubbly and sung loudly enough I pity the passersby. In his true buttoned-up fashion, Colin has listened intently, occasionally cracking a smile, but he hasn't deigned to sing along.

He never was one for big, showy displays, which begs the question why he even bothered to come. Maybe he and Charlie really have stayed in touch. Clearly, they have.

Obviously enough, he managed to keep in touch with at least one person from his past he's not related to.

It shouldn't feel bad to think about that, but it does.

I hate that it does.

We file out of the limo, a representative from the hotel escorting us to the event space. There's no way everyone gets this treatment—it must have something to do with the fact that Lindy's dad is a high roller at the casino here and is likely paying out the nose for the venue.

Inside, they announce Lindy and Charlie, and we all enter the ballroom to the sound of applause and cheers. I'm not sure how, but most of the guests managed to beat us here on the shuttles provided from the hotel to the chapel. The DJ immediately strikes up a song from Lindy's nineties boy band hits playlist, and the dance floor fills with people jamming out to Backstreet Boys' "As Long as You Love Me" as waiters pass drinks to anyone with a free hand.

That's how I end up sipping a third glass of champagne on an empty stomach. My head's a little fuzzy and I laugh easily, but so far, I feel great. Just lighter. A little freer.

"It's good to see you, CP."

My head whips around to see Colin sip from a highball glass filled with liquor that matches his eyes.

My oh my, he thinks he's cute using that nickname. He should realize he has no right to it, not after everything. And by everything, of course, I mean absolutely nothing in years.

But today is Lindy's day, and I can be civil for a few hours.

"You, too, Vicente."

"Last-naming me?" he asks, as though he actually cares.

I roll my eyes. Nope, civil's gonna take a hike. "What, are we supposed to be friends?"

His gaze narrows. "I've known you forever. Of course we're friends."

Hmm. Does knowing someone for the vast majority of one's life mean you're friends? I might've said yes once upon a time, but that fairytale came to a screeching halt when my faithful friend-slash-Prince Charming turned out to be a ghosting turd.

Yeah, a turd. Not a toad. Because a toad might be worth kissing, but the other one gets left to himself because he earned it.

"Are we really doing this?" I resist the urge to cross my arms and pop a hip for emphasis.

"Doing what?"

"Pretending like we know each other after not speaking for a decade? Come on, Colin. Be real."

He takes a long breath, then a sip of his drink, all the while studying my face with that unreadable gaze of his. After an interminable beat, he shakes his head, and a warm hand grips my upper arm.

"What if I said I regret every second I spent without you?"

Wait, what?

How dare he?

But at the same time, what?!

It's fair to say this is the moment the night shifts into something entirely new.

CHAPTER TWO

Colin

Janie Gruff is the kind of woman people say is beautiful and others instantly agree. But they have no idea.

This woman is downright gorgeous. Yes, she's got the long, dark hair and the olive skin and piercing blue eyes. Her legs go on for miles, and she has this freckle just under her left ear I spent a lot of time thinking about back in the day.

Back when I wanted her so much I could hardly think straight, but knew with every fiber of my being I couldn't have her.

"Every second, huh?"

She's studying me like she might be able to see through to the heart of me. A sadistic part of me wishes she could. Then she'd know exactly how I felt and still feel about her. I only needed seconds in her presence to know my preoccupation with my childhood best friend has gone nowhere, and the last hour has been ample time to confirm it.

I've kept my desire for her—my *need*—locked away. I never let on, not once, especially after graduation. I never came crawling back begging her to look at me and tell me we could work.

I knew we couldn't.

Janie and I are from different worlds, and even though I know if I said it out loud right now, she'd be furious at the notion, deep down she'd have to admit it. I had to, and it'd felt like someone had ripped out my heart when I finally accepted that I would never be good enough for Janie. My CP.

Coming from her parents, she shouldn't be so sweet. So kind. So completely lovely in every way, and yeah, I've probably idealized her over the years, but my mind didn't exaggerate how much being near her affects me. How being anywhere close to her makes all my logic and the reasons I can't have her collapse into a crumpled ball on the floor.

"Every second," I finally confirm. Because that is a truth I'll give her in this bizarre version of reality.

Since the moment I boarded the plane from Munich, I've sensed something coming. Some shift in me, or the weather, or whatever else might change the atmosphere or experience. That nameless feeling rode with me across the Atlantic and then across the country until I touched down in the desert and hustled to the chapel to see my friend get married.

It made sense the minute I walked inside and saw her.

The possibility I might see her had crossed my mind, but I'd refused to ask. I didn't want the mix of hope and dread all the way here. Now that I'm standing here, palm cupping the smooth skin of her arm, that sense of anticipation I couldn't have verbalized for all the world makes sense.

"Then why?"

She doesn't need to spell it out because I know. She means, *"Why did you leave me?"* and *"Why didn't you call me back?"* and *"Why didn't you ever return a single email or letter I wrote you?"*

I can't tell her it's because I was in love with her and still am. I don't want to tear myself open and lay all the broken pieces at her feet, and I won't. It's too much, and selfishly, I don't want to cry at my friend's wedding.

I can't say that I read and reread every word she ever sent me. That sometimes, I'd see how long I could go without reading one just to have the anticipation last a little longer, and to delay the guilt I'd end up feeling when I didn't respond.

I won't mention how much it hurt when I realized she was writing less often, and then how it cut when it all stopped. How I knew it was my own fault and I'd done it to myself—to both of us. But I also couldn't continue to let my heart and hope center around her. I had to make a life for myself, and I couldn't do that if I was constantly looking back at her.

But I can tell her a bit. Enough to ease the ache in me and maybe patch up some of the wounds I left her with.

"Because I was scared and stupid and I still am." There's honesty.

And Janie, beautiful in form and heart, shakes her head. "No, you weren't stupid. I'm sure you were scared. I..." Tears glisten in her eyes. "I missed you so much."

And then she steps into my arms and she's hugging me.

My brave, sweet, amazing CP is hugging me like these years of distance haven't torn us in two. She's hugging me like she can forgive me for being the worst friend to her, and I'm holding her back, indulging in the fantasy of this night because I know I won't ever have it again.

I'm deploying in a matter of days, and this woman's soft scent, the strength of her holding me and letting me hug her back, has all kinds of wild ideas running through my mind.

It may be true that I'm still stupid and scared, but Janie has always made me brave, too. And I wonder if maybe tonight, I can let that guide me, at least until we part again.

CHAPTER THREE

Janie

His scent is familiar, but new. He must use the same soap or deodorant. It has been so, so long since we've hugged, and I should pull away.

I am pulling away.

Watch how I pull away.

Finally, I step back. Because I might be a little egg cracking open, the white slipping out, but I'm keeping the dang yolk intact.

"Will you dance with me?" He holds out a hand.

I take it before my brain can even register my answer is yes. Because with him, even with this fully grown man, my answer is always yes.

If it weren't for the loopy little butterflies winging their way around my chest and the fizzy elation of the wedding, having him talk to me again, and yes, several glasses of champagne, I would be more circumspect. I just know I would.

How's a girl supposed to resist him when he says he regrets being away from her? Like, what phantom willpower should possess me and give me a strength I've literally never had? Not where he's concerned, anyway.

He pulls me close right as one song slips into another and our eyes lock as we realize this must be Lindy's playlist because the dulcet tones of *NSYNC's "Under My Tree" begin and we hear her cackle from across the dance floor.

"That one's a nut and always has been." Colin's voice is full of fondness as we watch Charlie and Lindy begin an awkwardly slow waltz to the odd and more than a little creepy Christmas song.

Charlie and Lindy went to Colin's high school, but Lindy ended up at college with me.

"It is super catchy. I remember belting this one out for years." I still would, if I could carry a tune at all.

He shakes his head slowly, a smile pulling at his lips. Which I am not looking at. At all. Because that'd be weird.

Friends don't look at friends' lips like they want to taste them, Janie, dear.

"I remember that, too."

I cringe, but I don't actually care. I long ago accepted I'm tone-deaf. "Apologies."

"I didn't say it was a bad memory. Pretty much all of my memories with you are good."

His hands were gently placed at my shoulder blade and cradling my palm that's not resting on the shoulder board of his uniform jacket, but when I ask, "Pretty much?" he curls me closer.

The light pressure of his touch settles into the curve of my lower back, and I can practically hear the rough callouses on his fingers rasp against the silk of my brides-maid's dress.

Okay, that's a bit much, champagne brain!

But also... *Ahhhhhh!*

"Any with just you are all good."

A breath gusts out of me, and some of the sparkly, happy feeling of being here with him seeps out because I have a strong guess at what he's not saying.

"My parents? After..." I won't say the words. If he's anything like he used to be, he won't want me to.

His jaw hardens, then loosens when he nods slightly. "Yeah."

My heart squeezes, maybe harder than it did when I saw him earlier. I know exactly the memory he's thinking of. About a week after his dad went to prison, Colin came to my house, but I was late getting back, and I walked into the entryway to find his head bowed unnaturally low as my dad glared at him. They'd clearly exchanged words. I knew in my gut my father had said something horrible to him.

Colin refused to tell me what he'd said.

"How are they? Your family?" He knows I mean everyone but his father.

"Mom's great. Busy. And Lina and Bianca are good, too."

He shares the news that he has nieces, and I know this already because I ran into Bianca at the market near my parents' house two Christmases ago. Hearing it from him makes me so happy, and yet there it is, that grief that threatens to edge out the joy of being back with him.

The reality begging to check this fantasy of a night. It's knocking at the door of my mind, whispering through the cracks, saying, *"Remember how he left? Remember how he never looked back?"*

JC Chasez is belting it out now, and I use his vocal prowess to bolster my determination—I cement over the door so I can't hear the whispers, and take a golden flute of champagne when a server walks by.

Because what bad things can happen with more champagne? *See? Fun! Yay! Happy!*

"Don't mind if I do," I say, winking at him like having too much champagne is my usual.

A party girl, I am not. But I also don't want to drown in the reality of our past. I want to enjoy the fact that he's here, holding me, *finally* talking again after so long.

We keep dancing to all the hits—Backstreet Boys, 98 Degrees, even an O-Town hit, and then all the Mariah Carey Christmas anyone has ever wanted, and then some. He matches me step for step, and we only break for a few minutes to go through the buffet line. I'm not particularly hungry, but I'm self-aware enough to know I need something in my belly to help the absolute ocean of bubbly in there.

"I've always loved this about you," he says, his eyes a little lazy and his smile lax.

We're both feeling *good*. And it's fun. And he loves something about me?

"What?" Because boy, tell me *right now*. I will collect all these shiny little pieces of sea glass he offers me while I can get 'em.

He finishes chewing a bite of his food while I wait. Nothing shall distract me from whatever he's going to say.

"The fact that you are this completely demure woman from an uptight home but you can put down food like a linebacker."

I gasp, then nearly choke on the giant bite of dinner roll I took, and we both crack up. This exact thing has happened more than once when I was shoveling food as a teen, and the floaty sensation making me feel like there are wings attached to my lungs is directly related to the fact that he remembers this about me.

He still knows me. Of course this is a small, silly thing, but maybe he means what he said. Maybe he does regret the time we spent apart.

It makes me so dang happy, and a little sad.

No. Not sad. Not at all sad.

Only happy.

"Only happy things tonight," I finally whisper to myself while he goes to get us waters and, yes, more champagne.

We'll relive all the fun silly things, and it'll be perfect.

We'll dance and laugh, and I'll inhale his scent and store it in the recesses of my memories. I'll write over anything sad and replace it with this night.

It's after midnight, and the party is winding down. We've dined, we've danced, we've watched Lindy and Charlie feed each other cake, then kiss with crumby, frosting-coated lips. It's disgustingly cute, and my heart has grown three sizes just witnessing it all.

Colin hasn't been more than a foot from me. When a groomsman cuts in to dance, the guy lasts for no more than a minute before Colin cuts back in, claiming me as his partner again.

I have absolutely floated through this night. My brain is fizzy and a little foggy and basking in so much happiness, I can hardly think about anything but these good feelings.

We blow bubbles as the newlyweds rush out of the ballroom and off to celebrate alone. We cheer and whistle and some of the groomsmen holler out comments about Charlie finally becoming a real man, and Colin and I laugh and grin at each other like loons.

Until his face falls a touch, the edges of his smile wilting enough to tell me his thoughts have shifted.

"I don't want to go yet. I don't want the night to end."

His voice is low, and he's holding my hand. Our fingers are twined in a way we never would've dared as teens. We're both a bit breathless from cheering. His hair is a little messy in front now, and he shucked his uniform jacket a while ago. My hair is sprouting wings around my face, and I'm sure my makeup is a mess by now.

I almost laugh, I'm so relieved. "Me, neither."

I'm pretty sure I never want this night to end.

We're together again.

He's here. With me. Again.

And we've had so much fun.

So we won't let it end.

CHAPTER FOUR

Janie

I wake with the feeling of a knife lodged into my skull. Someone must've broken into my room and attempted to off me, but they couldn't do it right away and gave up.

Or it's the consequences of my very uncharacteristic actions last night coming to call. *Fun.* I was never big on drinking much so I must ask the back of my eyelids if it's necessary to feel like one half of my brain is being severed from the other in the wake of imbibing a touch too much.

I had one too many glasses of champagne, yes. Not my usual choice, but when in Vegas for a friend's wedding and working off an empty stomach, what can one do?

Okay, fine. Maybe two *too many.*

And when an almond allergy hampers your best-laid plans to eat your body weight in cake, plus the nerves accompanying seeing your old crush again for the first time in a decade flare hot, things happen.

A rumbly moan sounds next to me, and I freeze.

Not any moan, but a very masculine one.

Fear streaks through me, and I jump out of bed with a shriek.

He jumps out, too, flinging himself to the other side with hands up.

And then it registers.

Him. Not just anyone in that bed next to me, but Colin. With no shirt on.

And no slacks.

Just a pair of black boxer briefs and miles of very grown-up man skin.

What did he do to get all those muscles?

"We did it," he says, hand running through his hair and chest heaving in the wake of the absolute jump scare we gave each other.

"Did what?" I ask, more like yelp.

Then it clicks. We woke up in the same bed, and he's nearly naked. My gasp is so loud, I wonder if I swallowed all the air in the room.

"No, not that, CP. You're still fully clothed."

The irritated grumble in his voice has me glancing down at myself, patting along my dress to confirm the presence of the miserable strapless bra and yes, all other underthings intact. It's all there. So unless we did things and then got me back into my shimmery gold bridesmaid's dress, maybe we didn't.

And honestly, wrestling back into the shapewear and strapless bra wouldn't have been on my list regardless of the scenario, so I'm confident there were no shenanigans.

This isn't a surprise. The other option would be... I'm not the "jump into bed with someone" kind of gal, especially not someone like Colin, whose entire life is pointedly about *not* sticking around. Thanks but no thanks.

The smoke clears from my head, and I'm lost trying to figure out what the heck is going on when a glint catches my eye.

A glint of sparkle on my...

Left.

Ring.

Finger.

My heart drops low, and it's not a gasp this time. It's full-on hyperventilation.

"Yeah. That."

My attention jerks up to see him tugging on the pants of his uniform. We're in my room, I realize as I spot my carry-on bag by the nightstand and a few things hanging in the closet. These details come into hyperfocus, right along with my shaking hands and the chip in my nail polish on my left pinky.

I sink down onto the end of the bed. "Wait. No. What are you saying? What happened?"

But as I ask it, the memories come in clips.

He's talking to me, telling me he regrets staying away, staying silent.

He's giving me those eyes, sliding a hand around my waist and asking me to dance.

He's telling me I'm beautiful. How he's always thought so.

He's leaning down and pressing a kiss just below my ear, then lower—seducing me on the dance floor there in front of Elvis and everyone. And I'm falling for it.

He talks about where he's been—all over Europe, some time in Korea, deployments to three different countries during two wars—he makes me tell him everything about my family's disapproval of my design business and how my brother caved to exactly what they want while I can't bring myself to.

I admit how lonely I am.

He says he is, too.

And it's not clear who has the idea first in the memory, but we both do it. We run off to the casino chapel and get married, sharing our first-ever kiss and one I wish I could remember a little better.

It'd be a fairytale if it were someone else's story.

In the here and now, I sink to the floor and tuck my face into my knees. "This isn't real. This isn't real."

"You in the habit of having waking nightmares?" he asks, the rustle of the fabric of his shirt brushing against his skin blaring in my ears.

I glare at him. "No. I'm not. But I'm also not in the habit of having a thousand glasses of champagne in one night and marrying someone I hardly know!"

He laughs, but there's no humor in it. "You know me, CP."

My teeth grind together as my jaw locks. He looks away, buttoning his shirt.

"Why did we do this? It's not actually real, is it? Like, there's a marriage license we can just tear up or something, right?" I know this is a reach and the closest to a tantrum I've had since I was a child, but I can't accept this. I can't process it.

He's reading something on his phone now, shaking his head. "We got the marriage license at the county clerk." His hand runs over his head again. "It says it might take up to a week to file it, though, so maybe we could head them off at the pass?"

My gaze drops to where he's buckling his belt, the taut skin of his abdomen a long stretch against the waist of his pants, which is a bit much to be filling my brutalized brain with so I jerk my head away.

"Right. Of course. Or, worst case, I'm sure my family's lawyer can get it annulled." The thought of my family finding out about this at all makes me want to shrivel up and die, but we could figure it out.

Honestly, more than one thing is making me feel that way. The strapless bra trying to strangle me. The Spanx still suctioning me into unnaturally smooth lines.

The memory of his chest and how insanely hot he looks despite how upset I'm feeling because my heart is a sucker for this man no matter what, apparently.

He yanks his phone out of his pocket and swears softly. "I'm barely going to make my flight."

I jump to my feet. "You can't just leave again. We have to figure this out. Seriously, Colin, no." My voice is shaking, so instantly furious I can hardly see straight. My brain whines from the sudden movement as I insist, "You cannot leave."

He stalks forward and takes me by the shoulders. His grip is firm but not painful, and he's looming over me in a way I can't help but enjoy. As little as I know him now, I know in my bones he'd never hurt me, and as a woman who's five-ten, I rarely have the pleasure of feeling small next to anyone aside from my brother and cousin.

I always liked how tall he is.

"I have to leave. I'm deploying in three days and got special leave to come to this wedding after promising no issues. I can't afford to miss my first flight because I have to get back to Germany. I'm sorry to leave you with this, but you can email me or whatever you need to do. If you need help, get ahold of my mom and she'll do whatever you need."

His brow furrows, and his gaze flickers back and forth between my eyes. My heart is absolutely thundering and I'm about to lose my grip.

Right, he's just going to leave. Again. Anytime something happens, anytime we get close—or I think we do—there he goes. He ups and bails.

"I'm sorry. This never should've happened. It's on me." He leans down and kisses my cheek, then pulls me into a hug.

As his arms close around me, they also squeeze all the anger out of me.

It's weird and stupid to want this hug, to need it, but I do. Because as much as I don't want to be married to him, I'm more than a little heartbroken. That's nothing to do with the marriage, though, and more to do with feeling like he's leaving me again. *Again.* We haven't buried all the hatchets, but we buried a few, haven't we?

"It's on me, too," I say, barely a whisper as he pulls away, missing the warmth of his skin and his mint-and-laundry-plus-warm-male scent even though it makes no sense at all.

He pauses at the door, that handsome face now stubble-rough and likely technically out of regulation. I wait for something from him, some word or emotion that will patch me up and make all of this better, somehow.

It wouldn't take much. I'm convinced. Just something. *Anything.* I don't even know what I'm hoping for but I'm certain it has to come from him and it has to happen now. After all of this, I need some sign that this wasn't all a stupid, wild mistake he'll regret when he's ten steps down the hallway.

And that I'll regret for even longer after he goes.

He hesitates, something earnest in his eyes, but after a beat, he shakes his head, gives me a small nod, and he's gone.

The door shuts behind him, and I do not cry.

I have given this man all the tears he's going to get, and the edge I skated, the hope welling in me that he'd do something to make all of this a little less like an ending, is gone. The woman who has been here, done this, steps up and firms her resolve.

No tears. No regrets. Just facts.

There's a post-wedding brunch for the bridal party at noon, and I have forty minutes to turn myself to rights.

What I will do? Show up looking great and not wallow in what just happened. I'll focus on my friends and their new marriage and what a great party they had.

Yeah, so great, it inspired you to get hitched, too!

What I will not be doing?

Letting on that I'm also now technically a married woman. Nor will I be dragging my sorry butt to the Clark County registrar to beg them not to file our marriage license. I may be strong, but I don't have that in me today.

Yet again, I've watched Colin Vicente leave.

Yet again, I'm picking up the pieces.

But this time, I know I can handle it. Might be a bit messier than before, but I can do this, and I'll do it without panicking and without shame. I'll get home, get it annulled, and let his mommy dearest deal with whatever needs to happen on his end.

He can fly back to Europe and deploy to war or whatever—no problem. Not something I'll worry about. I'm inured to worrying over him or even thinking about him anymore.

I'll live my life, and he can live his. Maybe we'll see each other down the line and have a good laugh about that one time in Vegas.

Right?

CHAPTER FIVE

Colin

Five years later - NOW

My new commanding officer is, for lack of a better term, jovial. He's Santa in human form if Santa was a fit man in his late forties with salt-and-pepper hair, no belly or beard, and a job as a colonel in a small unit in DC no one's heard of instead of the most famous gift-giver in the world.

"You're all set for the security interview next, right?" he asks, a downright cheery smile springing off his face the second I nod.

"Yes, sir. Twenty minutes. They were great to schedule me so soon after arriving."

My security clearance will expire in a few months

which means it's time to go through the hoops of the security interviews. They have all my paperwork, bank account balances and debts, foreign associations and travel, and of course, several character witnesses who've been interviewed.

It's a little more intense this time around since, as I've gained rank and positions requiring more intense background and security checks, I'm now working with top-secret compartmentalized clearances. Maintaining such access is imperative to not only my current work, but my future ability to progress. If you can't get clearance, you become useless.

It's not a big deal, but I'm always a little antsy walking in. I have nothing to hide, but I'd rather not deal with it at all. That said, I understand why it can't simply be an algorithm scrub of your life or an all-digital interview.

So, after wrapping up with Colonel Gleeson, I gather copies of all the paperwork I submitted weeks ago just in case I need to reference anything, and I head to the official interview.

The interviewer is cordial enough for someone who's combed through my personal information and interrogated my colleagues and former bosses about my integrity and values. And yes, that's dramatic.

Am I worried my dad will come up? Sure. Of course. Having a felon of a father who abandoned you and your mom and sisters and has continued to have run-ins with law enforcement can be seen as a liability, or even a security risk. I've created clear boundaries in this relationship and those are outlined for the interviewer, so we sail right past it all, thankfully.

We're wrapping up, or so I think, when he squints down at the paper and folds his hands on the desk.

"There is just one thing I wanted to ask you I don't see much about here."

Something in his tone nudges my pulse into a steady thrum.

"I'm an open book. Whatever you need for your investigation," I say, supremely confident I have nothing to hide.

He nods, seemingly relieved. "Well, I wondered why you haven't ever enrolled your wife in DEERS."

My heart stops for a moment, before my pulse crashes. "My wife?"

"Jane Elizabeth Gruff. You two were married five years ago in Vegas, based on the certificate. But you haven't ever enrolled her in DEERS."

He waits.

Bless him. Because my brain has jumpstarted and is running to catch up.

My wife.

Not my ex.

He's got our marriage certificate but clearly, nothing about an annulment or divorce, which should've been easily discoverable. I didn't disclose any of that because, again, it has been years.

But me sitting here acting like I had no idea I'm married will, to say the very least, *not* look good. So I force a low chuckle like it's the funniest thing.

"Janie insisted I didn't. She knew we'd be living separately while I was overseas due to her business here in the States and made me promise not to." That doesn't exactly make sense, but it's something.

"She didn't want the insurance benefits? You didn't want any of the housing or subsistence money that would come from having a dependent?"

He's suspicious now, and it's bad news.

Except there is some truth here I can use for this moment. "This is a little awkward, honestly, but, frankly, Janie is extremely wealthy. As is her family. She didn't need any of the money and felt uncomfortable with our receiving any benefits from the government when we have no need."

Investigator Wilcox's eyes widen, but he begins nodding slowly. "Ah, well what a lovely problem to have."

I laugh, a little relieved but not off the hook yet. "Indeed. I'm a very blessed man." Who has never wanted to roll his eyes *at himself* more than this moment.

"I do have to suggest you enroll her to, at the very least, simplify the process of survivor's benefits and such. She's not even listed as your emergency contact, or—"

"Ah, yes. Since I was overseas, it didn't make sense for her to be the contact, but I'll get that changed now that I'm back stateside." I shake my head at myself like it's one more thing I've forgotten to do since moving back. "Have you been OCONUS?"

He closes the folder in front of him and toggles the mouse on his computer before clicking through a few screens, presumably closing out my files. "Never did get abroad. Always wanted to live in Germany but just never got a shot. I'm sure the list is long when you get back."

"Yes. Even a bit of reverse culture shock after being away so long, but it's good to be home, too." It's not a lie, but somehow, I feel slimy about everything coming out of my mouth right now.

"Well, make sure you get to DEERS and take care of yourself, Major Vicente." He extends a hand, and I shake it, then leave his office.

I keep it together all the way to the car, then let my head drop forward to the steering wheel and a groan escapes as I walk through what I remember of the events years ago.

Janie and I got wrapped up in each other at the wedding and then decided to have our own. We got married and then ran back to her room, only to fall asleep, tragically and thankfully.

I'm conveniently ignoring the part where I let myself indulge in the fantasy of marrying the woman I've loved all my life even knowing it was foolish and potentially even cruel to the both of us. I do *not* want to linger on those thoughts and the accompanying feelings—*yuck*.

We woke up. She freaked out. In the light of day realizing what we'd done and how impossible it was to maintain and how completely surprised by it she was, I freaked out. We'd both been a bit out of it the night before, but we'd also both gone to the registrar and then the church. It had been a mutual decision.

But since I was already a solid hour later leaving the hotel than I should've been, I basically bolted. She said she'd handle the issue. Weeks later, my mom sent paperwork from a lawyer. I signed it and sent it back to her, which was a hassle considering my location at the time, but I managed. She confirmed receipt. And that was it.

And there it is.

My mom is an angel. She's dealt with so much garbage thanks to my dad, and she's been so proud of me and my sisters, but she isn't all sweetness and light.

Clearly, she never got the papers to the lawyer to finalize our divorce. And something tells me it wasn't an accident.

Does Janie know? She can't, can she?

Dread cramps in my gut when I think of talking to her, let alone telling her we've technically been married all this time.

I lean back against the seat and shut my eyes because I

have a second cruel revelation. I can't afford to look sketchy right now when I'm new to a unit, re-upping my clearance, and about to be boarded for my lieutenant colonel promotion. Suddenly popping up with a divorce decree sporting a weird date right after this could seem suspicious.

I've worked too long and hard to let a drunken mistake ruin my career. In some ways, it feels like it's all I have, and I'm not about to put it at risk because of my meddlesome mother.

So I'll talk to Janie.

It'll be fine.

I press a hand over the ribs on my left side where they ache, then mentally shove away the sensation.

I'll keep my heart out of it and it'll. Be. Fine.

Grabbing my phone, I type out the message to a number I haven't used in years.

"We're still married. Call me."

There. Abrupt? Yes. But no beating around the bush, that's for sure.

I wait and wait, then turn on the car because the cold has seeped through my uniform. DC's temps have dropped, and the late November chill has descended in full force. It's nothing like Germany's winter just yet, but the bone-deep cold of the humid climate is coming.

My phone buzzes and I watch the words pop up revealing something I didn't expect. Not outrage or confusion or annoyance. Instead, it's simple, and it's evidence she's thought of me far, far less than I've thought of her.

"Who is this?"

Mothers Of Military Network Message board:
> **Vic:** So...
>
> **JusticeLVR:** I'm listening.
>
> **SCLDG:** Out with it.
>
> **CoolyKay:** So..............
>
> **Vic:** I may have done something. A kind of bad thing but with delightful intentions.
>
> **SCLDG:** Again I say, out with it.
>
> **JusticeLVR:** Confession brings freedom, friend.
>
> **Vic:** My son got married in Vegas a few years ago. He deployed right after and when it came time for me to send in the finalized, signed paperwork on his behalf, I kind of didn't.
>
> **CoolyKay:** Okayyyy that is NEWS.
>
> **SCLDG:** I'm sorry but aren't you the person who has been lightly critical of our other various machinations and now here you are admitting you're a supervillain?
>
> **JusticeLVR:** That might be a *bit* of an exaggeration.
>
> **Vic:** I know. Trust me, I know. It's made the guilt worse, but also the hope. Seeing you all meddle and come

out with happy sons and wonderful daughters-in-law. I can't help but still hope.

SCLDG: Why tell us now?

Vic: He didn't know it wasn't finalized, and apparently neither did she...

JusticeLVR: Ohhhh.

CoolyKay: *Gasps* I need more information.

SCLDG: Keep us posted!

Vic: Will do.

CHAPTER SIX

Janie

This meeting will never end, and since I'm in charge of it, I should have my brain fully invested.

I shouldn't have sent that text. I shouldn't be pretending I don't know who's telling me we're still married like there's anyone else in the world besides Colin Vicente who could say that to me.

Alas, I did it. I couldn't resist, and I'm doing my best to let that suffice while I listen to this woman tell me all the ways she hates the design my firm did for her based on her very specific requirements.

The most fun part? All the things she hates are the parts of the design she *required* us to include. She wanted a black sink to accompany her black marble countertops—hates it. She wanted open-concept glass shelving with no cabinetry despite my suggestion to the contrary and, unbelievable surprise, she also hates that.

She hates the crystal cascade light fixture that had no business in a kitchen to begin with but which her friend found at an overpriced antique store and she just had to have.

She hates the blush pink carpet she insisted go in the dining room despite my every effort to dissuade her. She hates so much about the designing she did, and she doesn't see how it's all *her* choices. I don't want to sound like a jerk, but... *quelle surprise.*

My design sensibility tends to be fresh and classic. Especially in this area, you get a lot of people wanting an almost historical look. I use modern palettes with nods to the past and as much found wood and recycled material as I can. I like responsible design and economical options, which often don't click for the clients my parents send my way.

That's our détente—they'll loosely accept my chosen life of interior designer if and only if I serve their friends and connections. Then, they can take credit for any success I have, but still tut and shake their heads and say they "warned me about being in the arts" if something goes wrong.

It's great. I love it.

Especially when their friends are snooty clients who think they know what they want but, when presented with a design including what they've specifically asked for, turn their noses up or get upset because it doesn't look like my portfolio.

Of course it doesn't, Isabella. Your love of glass, black marble, and gold in mod-style angles doesn't exactly mesh with the softer, cozier style I hit. And it's not that we can't incorporate things clients want—that is, after all, a huge part of the business. But it never makes sense to me when someone comes to me and asks for something that is nowhere to be seen in my portfolio, I somehow manage to give it to them, and then they get mad about it.

This has happened three times in the last year, and guess who referred them all to me?

"You'll have to redo the color and we'll need to find other fixtures. I don't like the shelves like I thought I would, either, so we're changing those, too."

My stomach drops and the buzz of curiosity and irritation about Colin's text evaporates.

"Change the cabinets?" my assistant, Alice, asks.

"Obviously. I don't want open-concept so we can't have the glass anymore. Once the sink is changed out, the shelves will be all wrong." She studies her perfectly manicured nails. "You can't be surprised."

The smile spreading across my face is a sickly little thing and it's doing its level best to hide a genuine sneer.

"We are a touch surprised given how you selected them and approved them before they were hung." Knowing she'd be difficult from the first meeting, I've made sure we've gotten written approval directly from her at every turn. This way, we have a paper trail. But apparently, that doesn't matter.

"Well, I'm sorry if I couldn't visualize how they'd look in the actual kitchen. That's just not how I work. So you'll need to give me new options and I'd like the current ones removed—honestly, they're stressing me out and Marta doesn't like them either." She looks at her phone, then slots it into her designer purse.

Marta, we've learned, is her chef.

I feel for Marta. Truly.

"We can do that, but to be clear, this will add to the expenses and the timeline. We'll need to—"

"Aw, cutie, do I look like I care about the budget? Whatever you need, it's done. Just get this right for me, okay, sweeties?" She stands with her bag over a dainty wrist and twiddles her fingers. "I'll expect something by the end of the week!"

She parades out with an Hermès scarf trailing behind her. As soon as the door closes, Alice slides down in her chair and I slump, eyes glazing.

"It'll never end," Alice says.

"Never," I confirm.

This project is already a month over time and it's not because of my contractors or any industry delays. Those things happen—we order tiles or wallpaper or cabinets or whatever and the manufacturer has a delay or a ship gets stalled out somewhere on its journey. Maybe a slab of marble or concrete breaks in transit. We can't predict everything that could cause a delay.

But not this job. Not this special client.

My phone buzzes and my attention shifts to it to see Colin is calling me. A thrill of excitement and then dread hits and I shoot out of my chair.

"Getting a call and I need to take this. I'll be back," I say, running down the hallway to my office and shutting the door as though whatever awaits me when I answer is something no one else can hear.

"Why are you calling me?" I ask, more force in my voice than there would've been if I hadn't run through the halls in heels.

Although, no. I don't need to feel bad for the irritation in my voice. Yet again, this man has been all but a ghost in my life and then pops up out of nowhere to throw me for a loop. Sorry not sorry, I *am* annoyed.

"So you do know who it is."

The deep, almost rumbly masculine tone of his voice does not affect me. It just doesn't. I refuse to let it.

"Of course I do. Do you really think I have that many men who could say, 'We're still married' to me?"

Spoiler alert: I've only married one man in a drunken lapse in judgement for the ages.

"I have no idea."

This, maybe more than anything he could've said, infuriates me. "Huh, you know? You're right. You don't. Because you managed to marry me and disappear from my life in twenty-four hours flat."

I squeeze my eyes shut, hating the little wobble of emotion that snuck out at the end there. It's not indicative of a thrumming pulse or racing heart. It's not the sign of a deep ache punching up against anger and hurt. It's just the end of a long day.

He sighs on the other end of the phone. "I know. I'm an ass."

"No arguments here."

A beat of silence passes before he speaks again. "Can I see you?"

My heart picks up to a jog at the hopefulness in his tone. How am I so easily affected by him *still*?

"Just to talk. We've got to get this sorted out."

Oh. Right. Not to see me. But to figure out how to make the end of our sham of a marriage final.

"I'm free tomorrow at eight or Friday at four," I offer, business tone in full effect.

"Tomorrow. Tell me when and where and I'll be there."

Good. I'll control the context and hopefully that'll help. We'll get whatever needs to be said over with and I'll finally *finally* move on with my life.

"Andy's Place in Alexandria. Eight o'clock. I'll be with the cats."

"Uh, sure. I'll be there. See you then."

As close to home turf as it gets, and I'll have reinforcements. It does mean I'll have to tell Andy, and therefore also my cousin, what's going on, but at this point, it's way past due.

"See you then."

CHAPTER SEVEN

Janie

Andy's Place is my cousin's wife's cat café and it's adorable. I couldn't love it more, and she's already got it decorated for Christmas.

On the outside, it's cotton candy pink and has a big cat head for a sign with a steaming mug of coffee on top. Inside, it's a dream. The first floor is the café and bookstore. Andy's history of working at Alex Brews means she has some serious opinions about coffee and all the baristas trained to work here are experts.

But today, Andy herself is in residence, pulling espresso and steaming milk next to one of her employees, both clad in the signature T-shirt featuring the Andy's Place cat logo that says, "Come for the Coffee, Stay for the Cats." It's adorable and if I ever wore T-shirts, I'd wear that one. In the background, she's got soft, Lo-fi Christmas music going and has had since before Thanksgiving just like most of the city.

I'm grateful it's not "All I Want For Christmas Is You"—poor Mariah Carey needs rest after being thawed out for the season.

"Oh my, to what do I owe the pleasure?"

Andy's beaming smile greets me the second I step through the door.

"I have a meeting and decided to make it a cat meeting, if you have space." They took reservations for the cat space upstairs, but I had it on good authority they rarely had bookings for the earliest times of day.

"I can fit two, for sure," she says, pulling out a tablet where she keeps the scheduling software. After a few taps, she winks. "All set."

I fidget with my purse, nerves rising to the forefront now. Andy notices instantly because that's just the kind of person she is.

"Usual?" she asks, because I end up in here for coffee at least once a week.

"Yes, please."

She nods, then gets to work as I beg my nerves to settle. My knee is jumping under the table, but topside, I look calm and collected. Professional. The façade is one I've perfected over the years—I'm all shiny hair and smiles to those who see me for work. And that's who Colin will get today.

"So, what's got the knee bouncing?" Andy asks as she slides a coffee onto the table, then slips into the seat across from me.

I hesitate, but I need someone to confide in. It's not fair to ask her, but I do. "Can you keep this between us? I don't want you to lie to Will, but I need him not to freak out. I need to handle this myself."

Her cheery energy sobers a touch. "I can do that.

Maybe with the caveat that if you're in danger, I don't think I can keep it from him."

"I'm not. It's not like that." My feelings might be in danger of exploding everywhere the second I see the man, but Colin Vicente would never be a danger to me physically.

She nods, urging me to get on with it. I have maybe ten minutes before he'll be here, so here goes nothing.

"I'm meeting someone I haven't seen in a long time. The last time we were together, we got married in Vegas."

I avoid cringing against my own words and Andy's mouth drops open, then she slaps a hand over it and a muffled, "Continue," emerges from behind her palm.

"We did annulment paperwork after the fact—it was after a friend's wedding, and we hadn't seen each other and…" I shake my head, annoyed the memory still gives me a little twinge somewhere near my heart. "Anyway, he deployed days after from a unit based in Germany. So we didn't talk, and his mom took care of his side of things. I thought that was that, but he texted me last night to say that apparently we are still married."

Andy's hand falls away, her mouth still wide open.

"Can you not?" I wave at her gaping expression.

She snaps her lips closed and her lashes flutter. I see her getting a grip. Honestly, it's helpful to see her react this way because it *is* a big deal. I've resisted letting myself feel anything at all about the news, but the pull toward a hysterical spiral has been validated by her shock.

"This is just so not you. I mean, you never said a thing. No one knows, I'm assuming?"

Her brows have dropped and her face shines with concern for me. She reaches out and settles a hand on my wrist—a human connection for a beat before she withdraws.

"Yeah. Very much not me, and as far as I know, not him either." Not that I can pretend I knew him then nor do I now, obviously.

My heart squeezes. I'm already tired of the feeling.

"We have a lot of history together. And I certainly didn't want anyone finding out the failure of the Gruff family had gone and done something so stupid." I roll my eyes because I hate that it hurts to say aloud. I've done therapy for this, haven't I? I've processed the emotions surrounding my parents' expectations and their perpetual shows of disapproval while still acting like I'm one of them.

Andy scowls because she's familiar with the dynamic. In the year since she and my cousin married, she's learned a lot about me and the family's relationship.

"I know we're not discussing this now, but I can't stand how they treat you. It's absolutely stupid and it reflects on them, not you." She shakes her head. "I'm so sorry you had to deal with that alone."

I sip my peppermint mocha and take a moment to savor the minty-sweet flavor before admitting, "It was better that way. It helped to only deal with *my* feelings about it and not have to manage my parents', or even Chip's."

My brother and I aren't exactly close, but we aren't *not* close. It's hard to describe.

He did everything right according to our parents, and I'm the veritable black sheep because I chose the path I did instead of politics or non-profit management or even getting married right out of college and starting my duties as a trophy wife early.

Chip is the only one who understands why all of this hurts so much. Why it tore me open back when we were teenagers and Colin left with hardly more than a goodbye.

And that's exactly why Chip didn't need to know five years ago when we got married, or now.

"Well, I'm sorry. I—"

The bell on the door jingles and Andy's smile turns on. "Welcome to Andy's Place—Books, Coffee, and Cats! What can I get for you?" she asks, sliding out of her chair.

"I'm supposed to meet—"

A tall figure steps into my peripheral vision and I register it right as the voice says, "—Her."

I turn slowly, seeing the combat boots and uniform tucked into them sheathing long legs in camouflage pattern there's definitely a name for. My cousin Will would know. But Will can't know about this.

I follow the uniform further, the top featuring rank and the Vicente name tape, US Army on the other side and various patches I recall standing for one thing or another. It's less impressive than his dress uniform he wore to the wedding, but it's also formidable, somehow.

It's his face that gets me, though. He's clean-shaven and his dark hair is short on the sides and just slightly longer on top. His cheeks look thin, maybe, that jaw sharp and gaze sharper.

My pulse does a somersault and I'm grateful I'm sitting down.

"Oh! You're Janie's, um, her, uh, her meeting? I have you two scheduled for upstairs. Did you want a coffee?" Andy beelines for the counter and chats to him as she goes.

Bless her for drawing his attention away from me.

I focus on sipping my mocha, determined it'll imbue me with the courage and fortitude to face the man for an extended period of time. Because for some reason, seeing him like this makes me want to scream and cry at the same time and that is *not* productive.

I'm not falling for that, though. I'm not letting myself cave to the feelings. It's what I've always done, and I won't this time. I'll put him in the cat café and snuggle the kitties and get down to business with him. I'll maintain a professional air like I do with my clients.

I'll pretend he's Isabella's husband or something—he can be a snooty jerk to me, and I'll turn it around with a smile and deliver whatever they need to get the job done.

The only problem is, of all the things Colin has always been, snooty isn't one of them.

Plus, I have no idea what "the job" is right now.

CHAPTER EIGHT

Janie

Colin follows me up the staircase to the cat floor. I'm a touch self-conscious about him getting an eyeful of my rear, but also pleased I chose a very flattering pair of black slacks despite the inevitable downfall they'll experience thanks to the fur tornado ahead.

Take that, husband.

Just the thought sends a wobbly thrill through me as I step through the door and into the brightly lit room. The pink themes are more subdued up here—splashes of bright pink in decorative pillows or cat-themed artwork amidst white walls and furniture ranging from white to pale pink.

When Andy first shared her vision, I thought it strange, but the eclectic style paired with natural wood accents and ornate gold frames comes together in a charming, very Andy way. The smell is sweet and soft and speaks to how well they take care of the cats and the space, and of course there's a lingering coffee scent that gives it that cozy, homey feel.

"This is great," Colin says from behind me, his deep voice full of texture and grit.

When did his voice get so sexy?

"Welcome, you two. I'll get you settled and then, since you're my only two for the first hour, if you don't mind, I'm going to pop back downstairs."

Andy appears in front of us on the other side of a small child's gate. The old building has two entrances to the top floor, one for patrons and one for staff. It turned out to be a perfect design for the space.

"How many cats do you have?" Colin asks as I hang my bag and coat on hooks by the door.

"Right now, we have eighteen. We had a bunch of adoptions last weekend. We're getting some new kitties in Friday, which will bring us to twenty-three. I've been told by other people who run their cafés similarly that there's usually an uptick on adoptions this time of year, so we'll see." Her gaze casts toward a fluffy, grumpy-looking orange tabby who settles onto a squatty decorative poof. "Maybe even find Goob a home."

Colin's laugh startles me and I glance in time to see his face light up.

Oof.

Call me weak, but a man delighting in a small animal is basically poison to my efforts to hang on to the bad feelings stewing in my gut since his call.

"That cat's name is Goob? Do you name them?" he asks, washing his hands in the sink where I just did the same, attention on Andy.

"They usually arrive with names from the shelters. This guy was surrendered, and we've had him for almost six months now, but he's older and hasn't found his person yet. His full name is ridiculous so we just call him Goob for short." Andy crouches and pets the mangey fellow, who instantly purrs audibly, even from where I stand across the room.

Colin makes a noise that takes me back to when we were kids—this little clicking sound he makes as he holds out his hand to the elderly kitty in a way that might soothe him—and suddenly, I realize the error of my choice in meeting place.

I wanted the comfort of the cats and the relative anonymity that would come with being here rather than at a busy chain coffee place. Clearly, I'd also subconsciously wanted to have a reason to tell Andy, and in all honesty, a wayward part of me thought Colin might be off-balance surrounded by so many cats. Chip isn't a fan and with the exception of Will, I can't think of any male friend who has a cat.

But fool me watches Colin practically run to meet Goob while saying, "I need to know his full name."

Andy grins. "It's Gubernatorial Filibuster."

Colin barks out a laugh, jarring several cats whose responses range from ears perking toward him to protest-dismounting their current napping spots to gain space from the criminally disruptive man.

"Woops, that was loud. But... Gubernatorial Filibuster? Were they just trying to find the most obnoxious politically related names?" He ducks his head and runs two fingers over Goob's head between his ears.

It shouldn't affect me, but as always, it does. I should know by now anything with Colin will do things to me, and him being sweet to a raggedy old cat is no exception. This is the man who helped me rescue a cat who'd been hit on my street. We took him to the vet and turned out, he didn't seem to belong to anyone. I paid for the surgery to save him, visited him while he recovered, but I couldn't adopt him. It broke my heart to give him up, but my parents refused to let me keep him, and Colin felt he couldn't ask because his family was in the throes of a horrible time.

Of course he's still that man—compassionate and friendly... with cats.

"We haven't even been open a year and I've already had one Margaret Thatcher and one Alexander Hamilton. I feel like this is what it's like to have anything to do with anything in the DC area."

Andy and Colin share a smile as she stands, her attention coming to me.

"You two all set here?" Her brows raise high and make clear she's not just asking about being a patron of the cat room. She's making sure I'm okay being left completely alone with the guy.

Can I say no?

No. I can't. Even if I'm realizing I am the opposite of safe from Colin, who is currently nuzzling Goob's head with his forehead.

Wait, what?

"Are you about to adopt a cat?" I ask, nodding at Andy, who hustles back to the employee door and disappears. Normally, a staff member would be with us, but I'm basically an aunt to all of these little beasts, so we're getting special treatment.

"I wish."

He continues lavishing attention on Goob, and I decide to give him a minute before forcing us to deal with everything.

After another minute, a beautiful little gray tiger stripe I haven't seen before saunters up and takes an intrepid step toward me, one white-booted paw on my thigh. I greet him with softly spoken hellos before I realize Colin is watching.

My cheeks flush instantly and I don't let myself take in the expression on his face. It's too open and warm and it has nothing to do with me.

"So. We're still married?"

Smooth. So smooth, Janie.

Colin moves to sit at the other end of the couch I'm on, holding out a hand to another curious shorthair with mottled tan, brown, and white coloring.

"Apparently so." He sighs, then his gaze flicks up to meet mine. "I'm pretty sure it's an issue on my end, so I'll be looking into that. But first, I need to say I'm sorry."

I nod instantly. "Obviously, it's an accident."

"No, I mean I'm sorry it ever happened to begin with. I shouldn't have—I never should've let it get that far."

Oof again. Why does this hurt? It's so stupid, but it feels like someone twirled me around in shrink-wrap plastic and they're tightening it with every layer they pile on.

Had I pushed for it more than I remember? Had I been the one to spearhead the idea and he felt the need to indulge me, so that's why he feels this persistent need to apologize and take the blame? It's humiliating. The idea this falls at my feet makes me want to shrivel up in the cat tower.

I can't maintain eye contact as I say, "Oh, right. Yeah. Me, too. Neither. Whatever." *Great.*

He sighs. "I really am sorry, CP."

I stand, unable to sit so close and have this conversation like I don't care. Because I shouldn't care, he shouldn't be calling me that, and it's the anger and hurt simmering in me that has me pacing away from him toward a cat tree housing a cross-eyed Siamese mix of some sort and a sweet little peaches-and-cream tabby.

"Can we talk about this?"

I jump because his voice is *right* behind me, and when I turn, he's standing there, and he's holding Goob, snuggling the old fellow to his chest like a stuffed bear. Goob's motor is on full blast, his purr practically waving through the air, his little kitty face blissed out.

That must be the reason my heart aches to look at Colin. Definitely the cat.

I should tell him he's not supposed to pick the cats up, but Andy didn't give her full spiel since I'm family, and Goob looks more than happy to be where he is.

"Of course. That's why we're here." I move toward another setup, this time less a tree and more a castle with turrets swathed in cats.

"Will you consider staying put while we do?"

Goob's purr has followed me so I'm not jumpy when he speaks this time. Instead, I focus my attention on Bailey, a cat I've seen the last few times I've visited. She's got long black fur with a splash of gold like paint drizzled on her little forehead and wispy lighter fur floofing out of her ears. She's adorable, and the perfect distraction as she rolls her top half over and stretches her paws toward me in welcome.

"Of course. Say what you need to say. I'm listening."

I'm just not looking because I can't handle the sight of you with that cat clutched to your chest or the things my heart does in response, let alone all the messy feelings that've piled up over the twenty-five-plus years we've known each other.

"Will you look at me, CP?"

I grit my teeth, annoyed he's being so demanding and so *not* okay with him busting out the nickname already, but unable to deny him. When I give him my eyes, he drops his chin in a quick acknowledgement.

"I don't know how to say this any better, so I'm just going to say it." His brown-gold eyes courtesy of that uniform search mine.

I wait. I'm not giving him anything else, not even the need to ask me to turn around and look at him again.

"I need us to stay married a while longer, if you're up for it."

Of all the things I thought might happen today—me breaking down crying and embarrassing myself, or him acting dismissive of the whole deal, or maybe even discovering how we'd both managed to miss the fact that we'd been married all this time—this was not on my bingo card.

CHAPTER NINE

Colin

Janie was beautiful to me even when she had giant gap teeth and was so lanky it seemed like she'd never end up with the curves older girls had. But years later, in high school, she was the kind of pretty everyone noticed. Every guy in school had a crush on her, and yet she never dated a single one of them.

Talk about torture for a kid who knew he wasn't good enough but wanted her anyway—gap teeth or brace face or perfect, straight toothpaste commercial smile. *Title of my memoir*. It feels the same way now as it did then.

It felt the same way just looking at her while we said our vows, drunk on champagne and possibility and refusing to acknowledge the absolute idiocy of the move. In some ways, I couldn't fault the Colin of five years ago. He saw an opening with the woman of his dreams, and he went for it at an all-out sprint.

But seeing the surprise and confusion on her face now, reading the hurt lining her forehead and the way her lips don't turn up into a smile like they usually do. It makes me want to slap that short-sighted weasel upside the head.

"You... want to stay married. After apologizing for marrying me and saying you'll fix it, now you're saying you want to stay married?"

She crosses her arms, which I can tell she's been trying to resist. Everything about her actions so far today have said she doesn't want to seem upset by any of this, but she is.

I can't blame her. I'm the biggest jerk on the planet when it comes to her, and even if I have my reasons and always have, she doesn't have to understand them. *Plus, she doesn't even know what they are, genius.*

We may have skimmed over them in Vegas, but I've never spelled it out.

"That's the gist," I admit, shifting Goob so I'm cradling him like a baby in one arm. Thus far, he's perfectly content to relax in my arms which makes me even more baffled he hasn't been snapped up by a new family.

I have to appreciate the meeting location even more because focusing on the purring cat in my arm is a welcome distraction from the adrenaline crashing into my system as I prepare to convince her I need her help.

Janie studies her feet, a slight shake of her head sending my stomach to the floor.

"I'm not sure..." she trails off, then finally looks at me again.

She's hurt. I may not understand why exactly, but I'm sure at least part of it is that I'm standing here asking her to let me use her after not speaking to her for five years.

Yeah, genius, that could be part of it!

"Listen, I know this is crap. I know. It's a mess of my

own making and now I'm asking you to wade through it a little longer after you thought it was taken care of years ago. I'm truly sorry for that." I swallow hard, hating to admit this next part. "But if we divorce now, it'll look bad for me. Professionally. I'm at a critical point in my career. I'm about to be considered for promotion, and since I never mentioned any of this in the past, it's going to look like a security risk. I can't give them any reason to second-guess my integrity."

She blinks.

"And yes. I hear how bad that sounds." How can I not? I'm fully aware that asking her to continue lying about being married to me, or at least, not *stop* being married to me, is a move a guy with integrity wouldn't make.

But I've been climbing the rungs of this ladder so long, I don't know how to stop until I reach the top. *And if I never reach the top, I'll never be worthy of her.*

Not going to think about that right now, though.

I crouch to set Goob down on a cat bed nestled next to the castle, and to give myself some space to recover from that thought. From this whole reality, really.

When I return to standing, those brilliant blue eyes of hers are watching. My gut tightens and a memory flashes.

Her plush, perfect lips on mine as we stumble into the elevator.

Her body pressed to mine as I devour her mouth while we ascend floor by floor, oblivious to other passengers.

Our fingers laced as we run down the hallway toward her room, then burst through the door.

It ends in a flash when Janie of the here and now speaks.

"Can I think about it?"

She bends to run her hands over one of the sleeping cats

in the tower next to her. His yellow eyes blink open to watch her as she does it again.

Stupid to be jealous of a cat, but here I am. Every one of them garners her attention without effort while I can barely get her to look at me. Granted, she's always loved animals, always wanted pets though her family refused due to supposed allergies.

Even the one we rescued—a tiny guy she nursed back to health after he lost a leg, but her parents wouldn't allow it. Does she have cats now? Maybe a dog?

"Of course. Take a few days and let me know. I—it shouldn't be too much longer. But we can figure out the details of what it'd look like, if that helps. I'm stationed here now so I'm around."

I bite my tongue to keep from talking. I'm rarely this talkative, though with her I've never felt short on words. The babbling is a symptom of the desperation I feel, which makes me internally cringe and externally get a case of resting rude face.

"Okay." She exhales, gaze flitting left and right.

"Okay," I parrot, wanting to keep her here a little longer. "So, uh, how have you been?"

A ripple of confusion slides across her face before a humorless chuckle emerges. "We're going to pretend you care how I am, huh?"

The blow hits its mark. *Bullseye.*

I step closer to her, my voice low and steady despite the way her words have sliced deep. "I do care, CP. I—"

"Maybe it's time you call me by my name and not an old nickname that doesn't even make sense anymore."

The hits keep coming. "Whatever you want."

I'm not about to tell her I like her nickname, that I never want to give it up because it reminds me how close we used to be. But maybe that's exactly why she doesn't like me using it.

We stand there, both of us with eyes on cats roaming around and completely unconcerned with the walls between us, until I can't take it anymore.

"Are you doing okay, Janie?"

The words scrape out of me, a peace offering and a punch to my own face at the same time. Maybe I use her old nickname to avoid thinking of her real one, a name that's been tethered to some of my deepest hopes and most personal desires. But it's also one I have so rarely felt allowed to speak.

She stands after petting a long-haired white and gray cat with a pink nose, brushing her hands together. Her gaze searches back and forth between my eyes, looking for something she undoubtedly doesn't find. I have always been lacking, haven't I?

"You'll end up just like him, and I won't have my daughter associated with scum like your father. She's got a bright future and you aren't a part of that. You'll never be able to give her the life she's accustomed to. Best embrace reality now." Her father's words hurtle back into my head, and though I've made damn sure I'll never be like my father, both in character and in life choices, the sting of it still glitters in my memory.

She's never treated me like that, but I've proven it by leaving, haven't I?

"I'm okay. Are you?"

It's a simple question. I've had to ask it of myself more than once in the last few years, and my recent evaluation is a rough one. I can't tell her all that, not now when I've failed to make her believe I care even a little bit about how she's actually doing, and so I force a small smile. "Yep. All good."

Her lips press together in a move resembling a smile, but I swear broadcasts disappointment. She moves toward the gates where we entered and I follow, clear that no more conversation will happen today.

We lint-roll and wash our hands, and she bundles up. I don't have a jacket that's authorized with this uniform, so I have nothing to layer on as we descend. In the coffee shop, we wave to Andy, but she's got a solid line at the counter, and I wouldn't know what to say if we stopped to talk.

On the street, Janie turns. Her lips part, but there's a pause. I can't tell if she can't speak, or won't, and I've spent so long *not* communicating with her, I rush to fill the space between us.

"I'm sorry for all of this. Every bit of it." It's not enough, but I want her to know I mean it.

But just like before, this seems to force her even further away. Instead of relief or accepting the apology, she shrinks under its weight, and I'm left with only a tight nod of her chin before she mumbles something about being in touch.

I stand there like an idiot watching her walk away, wishing I knew what to say or do to make things right.

Reality is, I never can. Because I'm not sure what right looks like for her. For me, it's simply unattainable, and today has only served to remind me of exactly that.

CHAPTER TEN

Janie

Work kicks me in the already-sore shins as the day goes by like Frosty the Snowman sliding across a cheese grater made of asphalt.

Isabella calls three times. Alice and I are run ragged, but it's my shredded heart that feels it most. Why did I think starting the day meeting with Colin would be good?

I didn't. Not really. More so, I wanted to get the meeting with him over and move on with my life.

And how's that working for ya?

Obviously not well, since I'm slumping into my beautiful white couch, sweatpants on, hair wet from a shower, glass of wine in hand, and my mind is still running around the maze that is being married to Colin Vicente.

Not just that, though.

Being married, thinking I was divorced, finding out I'm still married, being apologized to like getting married in the first place was *all his fault*, and then being asked to *stay married*, as though all of that combined isn't the perfect recipe for emotional whiplash. Fun!

Oh, and now, he lives here. Like, for at least a while. So it's not just a neat little ambush and then he'll leave again. He's going to be close enough that even if I don't see him, even if he ghosts me again, I'll end up *feeling* and having to reckon with this mess far more often than if he would just head out to some other corner of the world again.

I want it to mean nothing to me. Why can't I be the kind of woman who falls out of love with someone they haven't seen in forever? How am I this feeble?

How does it feel so physically draining to stand next to him and look at him and feel the longing tearing at my chest and *know* there's no future there?

Maybe I should call Lindy and Charlie and ask them how *their* five-year-old marriage is going. They had a baby last year and they're reportedly tired, but happy. The wild reality that I've been married as long as they have, save a matter of hours is incomprehensible.

I won't be telling them about this, though. I have no idea if Colin and Charlie are in touch, but I doubt Colin will go blabbing it to him, either. They're tucked away in their balmy southern California life and it feels worlds away from the wintry chill descending on northern Virginia.

And on my life.

Okay now. Too much drama.

A text comes through and my heart flips, then dives when I see it's not from Colin. Not that I expected anything from Colin since I said I'd let him know what I think about the whole staying married thing, but I definitely have no interest in hearing from Barron Banks. *Ughghghg.*

Reluctantly, I swipe on the message and read.

"It's time we go out again."

No question. No "would you like to?" No effort at being charming because the child of my parents' best friends assumes I am his for the taking. About a year ago, he popped up and proclaimed he'd sown his wild oats and was ready for me. Literally, he said that. And I was supposed to jump for joy?

At the time, I'd coughed and nearly spit out my drink, then excused myself. A few weeks later, I got a text from him thanks to my dear parents since I certainly hadn't given him my number. They very clearly wanted to join our families, and since I hadn't successfully landed a man yet, they thought Barron Banks and I were meant to be.

I have no response to his text, so I set the phone down and take a long glug of wine. Another text arrives.

"I have to say it's getting a little old."

I sigh, then set down my glass and decide sure, I'll bite. I tap out, *"What is?"*

Seconds later, his response arrives. *"This little act where you pretend we aren't going to end up together."*

Now, this is the kind of thing that could sound sexy coming from the right person. An alpha male with a heart of gold who's always loved you and you're resisting? Sign me up.

No, really. Where shall I submit my signature?

A spoiled, rich egomaniac who genuinely believes you belong to him because he decided he wants you? Yeah, thanks but no thanks.

I don't respond to his message, and instead, open the thread with Colin after muting Barron's since blocking him outright would likely cause more drama than I'm ready for. This thought clicks in my head and it dawns on me there's no ending up with Barron if I'm already with someone else.

I feel more than a little angst cut through me as I tap out a text with a fluttering heart and a mind full of determination.

As if that's my only option... but it seems to be. It is. Or at least, it's the only thing I can think of, and it's sitting right here at my fingertips. *Sigh.*

"I'll do it, with some conditions."

He might not like what I plan to ask of him, but it's what I need to make peace with myself about this. To make all of this bearable. I hate that I'm feeling so tender, so I need to focus on what I'll get out of it. And nothing has driven that home more than Barron Banks's efforts at flirting.

Or maybe it's marking his territory.

Either way, consider me un-wooed. Anti-courted. Ill-charmed. All the negative prefixes.

The response from Colin comes in less than a minute. *"Anything you need. Can I take you to lunch on Saturday to discuss?"*

And though I'm not sure my reserves will be fully fortified by Saturday, I accept. I have no choice at this point. I have to face the situation, and if I'm doing this, I'm going to get something out of it besides scratched-open old wounds and a headache from gritting my teeth against tears.

Colin stands when he sees me enter the restaurant. He's always been punctual and no surprise, the military hasn't changed this about him.

Inevitably, he looks ridiculously handsome with his almost stern bearing and dark hair. His cheeks are dusted with stubble, so he must've skipped shaving this morning. It gives him a rakish appearance I do my best to ignore. He's wearing a long-sleeved dark olive-green Henley shirt with a few buttons at the top, the first undone, and jeans. There's a jacket of some kind hanging on the seat he just stood up from.

"Hello, Janie." He leans in and presses a lightning-fast kiss to my cheek.

I falter, caught completely off guard. I wasn't expecting this kind of intimacy, or even any at all. "Hi, Colin, um, hi. Nice shirt."

It is nice. The color makes his brown eyes impossibly vibrant, almost fully green, even in the pale wintry light of this early December day. The soft-looking material smooths over his pecs then falls straight and gathers a bit where the belt around his jeans juts out. If he's anything like he was five years ago, there's nothing but hard, ridged muscle under there.

And wow, I need coffee.

He pulls out the chair for me, and a stupid little thrill races from where his thumb brushes against my shoulder when I sit before he removes his hand.

"Thank you."

He slides into his seat, his expression lighter than it was when we parted two days ago. "So I'm thinking four months minimum, six if possible, but I'm open to discussion."

Logically, this isn't a surprise, but I still jolt. He went right for it, didn't he? It is, after all, an agreement we're making. He doesn't get in trouble with the Army and I become unavailable to Barron. We're not here for anything else. "Six months..."

The waiter arrives right as he's opening his mouth to say more. I'm disappointed, curious what he would've said, but eager for caffeine. We both order breakfast and coffees, and when we're alone again, he doesn't make me wait. Of course he doesn't.

"Could be four. Or we can play it by ear, if you're open to that. But I need to get past the holidays and the first few months of the year." His brow is furrowed, though he thanks the waiter when the man delivers our coffees, ever polite even when he's got that focused expression on.

Nerves knot in my belly, but I swallow a sip of coffee and say my piece. I promised myself I would take something here, and so I'm doing it. "Okay. I'm open to that. I'll just need something in return."

He nods instantly. "Anything you need."

I ignore the zing of hurt that nags in my chest because what I needed was for him to be a friend to me years ago and not willing to do whatever I ask now just to get what he wants, but I shake that off and explain. "I need you to attend my family party and pretend to be my date. Obviously, I don't want people knowing we're married or that would cause more trouble, but date should be enough." I hope.

Bringing someone who is *not* Barron Banks to the Gruff family Christmas party will ruffle Barron's feathers and likely put a dent in his ego. So far, he's been fairly impervious to my efforts to avoid him or shoot him down, but thanks to a few ambushes by my parents, we've ended up seated together and even dancing at a gala or two. Those instances have been enough for him to speak to me the way he does, with all that swagger and unearned confidence stating I belong to him.

A man like Colin on my arm will throw him into a tizzy. Just the thought brings a smile to my face, especially if I ignore the tiny flip of excitement that comes from the thought of Colin as my date. I don't need to worry about that because it'll be fake, and I'll keep feelings for my oldest friend and first crush tucked neatly away. I'll hardly see him except that night, and I'll know I'm getting what I need from him.

It should make me feel mercenary or slimy, and I'm sure if I stop to think about all of this, it will. But for now? I'm going to savor the thought of Barron Brat-face Banks getting soundly rejected without me having to say a word.

The imaginary bliss of that moment is ruined by the reality check of this one when Colin levels me with a look I can't read. After a beat, he explains.

"That's fine. Because I'll need you to come to a few events as my wife, and we'll need to make it look convincing."

CHAPTER ELEVEN

Colin

We've agreed to the terms—she'll come to a few events for me, and I'll do the family party for her. Now we're sitting here in silence while the rest of the diners enjoy their Saturday morning brunch and "Holly Jolly Christmas" plays over the restaurant speakers.

I keep waiting for Janie to break the quiet between us. She was always a chatterbox, and I was her captive audience regardless of the subject, but the passage of time has torn up those familiar traveled roads.

It might be self-aggrandizing, but I swear I can read strain and maybe a touch of the same hurt I saw yesterday still in her eyes on the rare occasion she meets mine. It occurs to me that she's asking me to be a fake date and isn't upset by all of this because she has a partner. It could've been far worse if she was serious with someone.

And the thought of that sends a familiar queasy feeling

through me. I can't keep thinking about someone else with Janie or I'll be sick, so I forge a new path between us.

"Are you still doing interior design? How's that going?"

She told me about her work in Vegas. For a guy who blamed alcohol for a huge, foolish mistake that night, I sure do remember every word she said to me.

Maybe it's easier to pretend you were drunk and not just a tipsy, lovesick fool finally confronted with the object of your long-held affections.

Yeah, no. I've shoved that thought into an ammo box, padlocked it, and chucked it into the sea.

"It's going pretty well."

Her gaze cuts out the window like she can hardly stand to keep sitting at this table with me, and I have to do something.

I don't want everything between us to feel so strained. So... obligatory.

I want her to want to be here. To want me. *What a waste of energy.* I can't manufacture that reality, but what I can do is try to repair what I've broken. At least a few of the cracks.

"Hey."

It's all I say, but her eyes slide right to mine. *Damn, she's beautiful.*

"I know it's too little, too late, but I need to say I'm sorry. Not just for the mess in Vegas and all of this, but for everything."

She doesn't respond, only waits, as though she knows there's more. She's not wrong.

"I disappeared on you. I honestly can't explain it other than to say I saw a way to make my life something it had never been, had never hoped to be, and I took it. I'm genuinely sorry it ruined things between us."

She'll never know how agonizing it was to keep from talking to her every second I was allowed to. To call home instead of her when given leave to contact family. To write letters to my mom instead of her.

To stay away when I came home for breaks. To keep from asking about her when my mom visited me for parents' weekend. To keep my eyes and mouth and hands off her when I saw her for the first time in years and she didn't slap my face for how I'd abandoned her.

She nudges one last bite of an omelet around on her plate before surrendering her fork.

"You're right. I don't understand. I wish I could." She dabs her mouth with the corner of her napkin, then sighs. "But I think I'm done with feeling bad about it. And if we're going to be convincing, we're going to need to at least be actual friends again."

Hope takes root in my chest. "Absolutely. Yes. We need to be friends."

Her friendship was the most valuable, precious part of my life growing up and missing it all these years is my primary regret in life. If we can navigate this marriage mess for a few months and repair our friendship in the process?

Ideal.

Her soft smile has another thought chasing that one.

Except you were never just friends.

"So other than being back in the area for work, what's going on in your life?"

Her question is casual, and if I didn't live inside my own head, I might believe we had cleared the air entirely.

But I heard her. She doesn't understand. And a huge part of me is roaring to tell her the truth about all of it.

Thankfully, my survival instincts win out, like always.

"Work is typically the majority of my life, sadly." I

laugh self-deprecatingly, but there's a pinch behind my ribs, too. I've never been more aware of how thin and sad my life is until this moment when I honestly can't tell her what I do besides work.

She's shaking her head, though. "I don't believe you. I mean, of course you work a ton. You've been very devoted to your career. But what about reading? And hiking? Don't tell me you didn't spend every spare second you had in Germany in the Alps."

Warmth glows in my chest like she plugged in the lights on a Christmas tree.

"I did hike quite a bit. I already miss the mountains." I lived a few hours west of the German Alps, and I escaped there every chance I could. Sometimes, I'd go to Switzerland or Italy, but the German and Austrian Alps gave me days of respite and clarity.

"We don't have those kinds of mountains here, sadly. But I guess you won't be here all that long?" Her gaze stays pinned on her plate.

I'm grateful. I don't want her to see me shift with discomfort at the question. "Likely, no. Depends on the promotion and a few other things. Maybe three years? More likely two."

I'm already antsy for the next thing—assignment, promotion, change—that'll keep me moving. At the same time, the sensation grates against a part of me that instinctively wants to stop and stay.

It's a feeling I have only ever had with her, and it's one that almost always instantly fuels the opposite desire to run.

"Well. I hope it's a good few years. And maybe it's long enough in one place to adopt Goob, since he's clearly smitten."

"I wish. He's a good guy. But what about you? Tell me

all your animals' names." She wanted pets so bad when we were kids.

Her face falls but she blinks away the change and takes a drink of water. "I don't have any. Yet."

The way she avoids looking at me gives me enough to go on, so I approach gently. "Why not?"

I don't want it to sound critical, because who am I to say anything about it? But I remember how desperate she was for a cat, and how she loved my family's dog, Corvo. She sobbed when he died my senior year of high school. She was sixteen and I thought she'd never stop crying.

With hindsight when I reflect on it, I think she was grieving both Corvo, the delight of a dog himself, and also her chance at having a pet nearby. She grew up with him as much as she could living on the other side of the fence that split her sprawling mansion grounds from my side of the neighborhood with a significantly different income bracket. She knew she wouldn't have another dog unless my parents got one, and likely wouldn't have a reason to see it once I was gone.

And once I left, I stayed gone.

"Honestly, I'm overdue. I think some part of me felt like I should wait until I was more settled, but how much more settled am I going to get? I own my townhouse in Alexandria; I have a business that's sturdy." She flashes a smile but it's not a real one. "It's time."

"Is that why you go to Andy's?" At some point, she mentioned she went at least once a week.

She shrugs one shoulder. "I also love Andy since she's my cousin's wife. The cats are a bonus."

"I think it's time. You were born to be a pet parent."

The smile growing on her face gives me heartburn, but I return it. I'm tempted to reach out and cover her hand with mine or adjust my legs so our knees brush—anything to create contact between us in this moment that has somehow broken through years of distance.

But the waiter slaps down our bill and ends the connection. Her phone buzzes and her expression darkens when she looks at it. She reaches into her purse and I know what's coming.

"This is on me," I insist, but she tosses down two twenties anyway.

"I'll pay for my own breakfast, but thanks," she says, rising from the chair. "I have to run."

I stand, hoping for something I can't name, but offer a nod when she gives me one last fleeting glance and heads out.

"I'll send you dates," I say, hoping she knows I mean dates I need her for work.

She gives me a little wave and keeps moving, out the door of the restaurant before I manage to pull out my own cash and leave it there. Decent service, but the guy's getting a solid tip because I don't want to be here anymore. *Not without her.*

As I leave, Janie nowhere in sight now, I can't help wondering just how many times I've had that exact same thought.

M.O.M. NETWORK

Mothers Of Military Network Message board:

Vic: He's coming for dinner. He's not happy.

SCLDG: Boohoo. Poor baby. His mother kept him married to the love of his life. Isn't that what you said? He's always loved her?

JusticeLVR: It's not that simple, of course.

CoolyKay: There's something to be said for romances that have history.

Vic: True. That's my perspective, obviously.

SCLDG: So don't worry about him not being happy—that's temporary.

Vic: We'll see. I worry.

JusticeLVR: Of course you do.

CoolyKay: Yes. That's natural. But you believe he deserves a life filled with love, don't you?

Vic: They both do. If they can manage to get out of their own way and actually admit their feelings, it can work. I know it can.

SCLDG: Tell him as much.

JusticeLVR: Yes, be honest. Maybe he needs someone to have faith in him before he can really hope.

Vic: Good thought.

SCLDG: And don't hesitate to get a little messy. Make sure they can't avoid each other.

Vic: Might need your help with that.

SCLDG: Say the word and I'll do anything I can.

JusticeLVR: Me too.

CoolyKay: Can't imagine how I could help, but I'm in too. We're all rooting for you—and for them!

Vic: We'll see how it goes!

CHAPTER TWELVE

Colin

My mother opens her front door, the same one I grew up coming home to every day after school, with a giant Rudolph-face-complete-with-blinking-nose sweater on.

Despite the kaleidoscope of crashing emotions after discovering she never finalized my divorce from Janie, a low-level ache eases when she pulls me into her arms. She's come to visit me a few times in Europe, often at Christmas, and I flew home once in the last few years. But overall, my relationship with her and my sisters has subsisted on texts and monthly video calls in the long stretches between in-person visits.

"I'll miss the Christmas markets, but it is so good to have you home."

She squeezes me hard, and guilt crawls up my neck.

I haven't been here. She'd come visit in December and she'd travel around to the markets while I worked, then we'd go together on weekends or evenings. It was good time together. But I haven't been home for Christmas in at least a decade.

"Good to be here, Ma."

She pulls back and looks me over, the routine familiar. This is what happens when you're the only son to a mother who has two daughters who live nearby. Even if we have cobbled together a decent amount of contact, she'll never be satisfied with it.

"You're thin. Have you been eating?" Her dark brows furrow in her pale forehead, though she looks great as usual. She's in her sixties but absolutely still kicking aging in the pants.

My sisters and I all ended up with dark hair thanks to both parents having it. We also ended up with my father's more olive-toned skin. Only Lina got Mom's blue eyes, and Bianca and I have our father's brown ones. In the end, we do look like we match, even if I'm well over six feet and my mom and sisters are all solidly under five-three.

"Aren't we supposed to avoid commenting on physical appearance?" I ask, remembering Bianca's lecture a few months ago when, on our family video chat, my mom mentioned she looked tired.

Her indignation wasn't out of place. Bianca has been tired for the last six years thanks to a husband who works all the time and three kids no more than eighteen months apart. She says she'll be tired for at least a century after she dies, and I don't doubt the truth of that.

"Oh, hush. I'm saying it to you because it means you're working too much. But now you're home and you're going to eat and take a breath." She takes a breath as though to prompt me to do the same, holding my forearms to keep me in place.

I humor her and take a large inhale, then slowly let it out. The cool air filling my lungs and the cold nipping at my cheeks is surprisingly refreshing.

"Good boy. Okay. Come in, and let's talk."

She turns and we enter the home with that same familiar set of smells—coffee, cinnamon, detergent, and whatever the Vicente family home scent is. The only thing I've mentioned about the divorce paperwork is the text I sent the day I found out earlier this week. It said, "So when you said you sent in the divorce paperwork..."

She responded with telling me to come to dinner today. So here I am. And there's no point in pretending I'm here for any other reason.

Yes, I want to see her.

Yes, I'm glad to be home.

No, we are not going to talk about anything else until I understand what happened.

Even if I am planning to stay married to Janie for a while longer, I still need the truth from my mother.

She leads me to the dinner table, the same one where we always sat for dinners my growing-up years. The same one where I did my homework while she cooked dinner.

The same one where she sat us down to tell us our father had been arrested. That he'd be gone for a while. We all cried, not understanding, not relieved by her promises he hadn't done anything violent, but had stolen from good people and had been doing it for a while.

The same one where I sat to catch my breath before opening the acceptance envelope from the United States Military Academy.

So many memories from my past right here, it's weird to

sit down to discuss something from my present, but here we are, sitting in our long-ago designated seats at the worn wood table. There she is, pouring out steaming herbal tea since it's too late for coffee according to her internal caffeine consumption clock.

When she finishes stirring in her squeeze of honey, she sets the spoon down and waits. Is she expecting me to chastise her, or maybe even apologize?

I sigh and hang my head. "Why didn't you send it in?"

The words sound more broken than I anticipate, but she grasps my wrist, so I look at her. I'm six and ten and seventeen and twenty-five again, looking to my mom to sew up my broken heart. Her face is lined with the trials of life, but she's got that determined squint in her eye and is shaking her head in a way that is so familiar.

"This right here is why."

Her voice is gentle, but she's shouting, isn't she? That's why it hurts to hear it.

"This, what? What does that mean?" I croak, hanging on to the shreds of my illusion.

Her head tips to one side and she radiates compassion when she asks, "Can we talk about it now?"

I pull back and scrub a hand over my face. Why did I think this whole visit would go differently? I saw myself walking in here, chatting for a minute, maybe, and then telling her she should've sent the papers. Maybe asking why but not going directly there.

But I'm thirty-four years old. Isn't it time yet? Haven't I been thinking of all the ways I wish things were different? And if so, what am I going to do about it?

Start here, I guess.

Summoning what little courage I have for the subject, I agree. "Yeah. We can talk about it now."

She sits up straighter, one hand holding her mug of tea. "You've always loved her."

I nod. There's nothing to add.

"So when I saw what you'd done—what you'd both agreed to do, I couldn't stand it." She frowns, lips pressing together so firmly they disappear before she continues. "You've loved that girl and never thought you were good enough. And I know you'll never believe me, but she has loved you."

I'm already shaking my head. "You don't have to—"

"Colin Riley Vicente, you must listen now."

There's a wobble in her voice amplifying her vehemence, but I can't move even if I wanted to.

Once she sees I'll stay quiet, she continues.

"You left because you had to and I don't know how you left it with her, but you're back, you're still married, and I'm going to tell you that if you have any ounce of feeling remaining for that girl, any whisper of hope that you might one day have a chance with her, you must take all that determination and grit and apply it to *her*."

I blink, stunned. I expected her to tell me I owe Janie an apology, not for her to give me a fight speech.

"That's right, I think you should try. And see. Because that woman is still single and she hasn't gotten close to any other man. If she had found someone and applied for a marriage license in the last five years, all of this would've come out."

With a sigh, I sip my tea and filter through possible responses. "Mom, I love you for thinking she might—"

"It's not just me thinking. I'm seeing proof. I haven't seen her in a decade but she chose to marry you five years ago, and—"

"Mom! We were drunk! We were idiots! We did something spur-of-the-moment while caught up in the moment at our good friends' wedding and the second we had a hint of clarity, we agreed it was foolish. Neither one of us had any illusions about trying to make it work." The words slide out easily, but they feel wrong. And I don't want to dwell on this feeling.

She takes this in but doesn't let it stop her, apparently, because she presses again. "Maybe so. But you're still married, and you've never had a better excuse to try."

I laugh and it's ugly and bitter. "Well, you'll be happy to know I asked her to stay married a while longer so I don't end up losing my security clearance after failing to disclose my marriage. She agreed to keep it up for another few months and even let me coerce her into showing up at a few events for work so it doesn't seem quite so out of the blue." There's an edge to my voice that shouldn't be there when speaking to my mom, but I can't hide it.

And she's not bothered one bit. She simply blinks in slow motion and grins. "Well, isn't that convenient."

My head drops back because she's not getting this, but before I can correct her, she launches in.

"My sweet, clueless son. This is perfect. You have an opportunity to woo her, to let her see the man you are now, served up on a silver platter. Take it." Her deep blue eyes pin me for a moment before she shrugs. "Unless you can really say you have no desire to see what happens."

The grin on her face doesn't waver because she knows she's got me.

I've loved Janie Gruff since the moment I saw her and I might've given up hope at different points in life, but the prospect of *not* shooting my shot if I've got one isn't one I can stomach. Not at this point, and not after so many years of assuming I had no chance.

Miraculously, instead of dread, there's a tiny grain of hope digging in somewhere, and for the first time in what feels like forever, I'm excited for something.

M.O.M. NETWORK

Mothers Of Military Network Message board:

Vic: It happened. And I think I might've gotten through to him.

SCLDG: Excellent work.

JusticeLVR: Yay! Christmas miracles!

CoolyKay: Hooray for you! Great work.

Vic: I told him he needs to try—if he's ever going to have a shot, it's now.

SCLDG: Sure seems like it's now or never after all this time.

Vic: Agreed. By the time he left, he said he would plan to try to see her before they attend the events they both agreed on. It gives me hope maybe they'll break through some of the ice before they're having to perform.

CoolyKay: I hope they do. Here's hoping!

Vic: Amen.

SCLDG: He's a smart young man.

JusticeLVR: Crossing my fingers for those sweeties!

CHAPTER THIRTEEN

Janie

Andy and Grace have been at my house for ten minutes when I finally blurt out what's happening. A regular at her cat café, it was only a matter of time until I met her bestie Grace who's married to Will's good friend Justin. And forces of nature they both are, they swept me into their group on the spot.

"So. He doesn't want to get divorced. He wants to stay married for a bit." I explain the security clearance and the new unit, his upcoming promotion, and I don't mention my feelings about this.

Grace chuckles, a sly grin on her pretty face. Her husband is at home with their daughter while she and Andy visit me. I gave Andy permission to tell her on the promise she'd give me time to tell Will myself—thus far I've been too chicken—so they're stopping by to catch up on the latest developments.

"You realize neither of us is in a position to judge you for staying married to someone for any reason, right?" Grace's kind smile eases me a touch.

"For real. I married a guy for insurance. This one married a guy for his apartment, basically." Andy's thumb points at Grace, who shakes her head, though I'm not sure if it's aimed at Andy or herself.

It's a good reminder for me, though. "I know. I feel bad. I'm using him."

"He's using you. You're both using each other. And yes, that doesn't feel great, but as long as you're both upfront about it, you might as well both have some benefit from all of this."

Grace's perspective is valuable. She and Justin had some connection before their marriage began, but they weren't in love.

Neither were Andy and my cousin. Theirs was an even more utilitarian start.

"What's really in there? I feel like you're not saying something." Andy pats my shoulder and she and Grace exchange a look.

It's meaningful in a way I can't decipher, but it cracks the wall I've thrown up and suddenly I'm explaining.

"You both married men you felt you could trust, but not that you had feelings for. Or, *positive* feelings for."

I raise my brows at Andy because I absolutely relish that she thought she hated Will before she realized what a sweetheart in disguise he is.

"It's just that I do. Have feelings. I always have. And not simple ones. Big, messy, *crushing* feelings. All of this is barreling toward me getting flattened when it's over and I —" I swallow, scrunch my nose to stave off tears, and exhale. "I don't want to go through that again."

This is where the real doubt comes in.

"This may be way off, but is there any chance—"

"No."

Andy is coming from a good place, but she doesn't understand. I can't let myself open to the possibility that this could actually become something, because I have all the evidence I need to prove it won't. It cannot.

Andy nods and Grace stays quiet, but they're still here, supporting me.

And then my doorbell rings.

"Is that him?" Andy whispers, and Grace laughs at her dramatics.

"I think so."

His work party is in a few days so he's stopping by today. He asked if we could go for a drink and I agreed. What else could I say?

I don't want to spend time with you because I'm scared I'll like you even more instead of focusing on what I can get from you and I really don't have time for that kind of nonsense in my life right now, kaythanksbye.

Ugh, the thought still makes me feel a bit gross, even if it's honest. They've reassured me it's good I'm getting something from this, but I can't help but feel this is all going to blow up in my face. Hopefully, I'm wrong, though.

Andy and Grace bustle toward the door and swing it open before I can.

"Hi."

Andy jumps in to respond. "Hi there, Colin. We met the other day at the café."

"Right. Great to see you again, Andy."

"And this is Grace. She's an amazing saint of a woman who is a school nurse, mom, and wife to a JAG officer who also happens to be my grumpy husband's best friend."

Grace and Colin shake hands as he greets her, then his gaze shifts to mine.

My insides fizz, which is probably a medical situation I should consult Grace about, but instead I smile. He smiles back and it's... Honestly, it should be packaged and sold as dessert. "Hey. Sorry. These guys were just leaving."

Andy scoffs but she's wearing a wide grin that says she knows how much I want to consume this man.

"Um, rude much?" She winks at me. "Actually, she's right."

Colin steps aside, and they toss farewells to us over their shoulders with arms linked, and I can only imagine the commentary in our text thread later.

If this were her house, I would've been nervous standing here in the doorway. I can almost guarantee she has mistletoe perched on the eave to catch unsuspecting couples, and I wouldn't put it past her to try to sneak some up at my own house, though she was never out of my sight so I'm safe for now.

I lock my door and turn to Colin, reminding myself we're friends and friends spend time together and getting to know him as he is now is a smart move for our future interactions and doesn't mean anything.

My mind is practically a run-on sentence as we head toward the center of Old Town.

"Did you have something in mind? I was thinking we'd grab a drink and then go browse the bookstore."

I trip over my own feet because I am all that is refinement and subtlety. And the bookstore? Really? "That's perfect."

We chat about nothing—the twinkle lights strung around every tree and lamp post, the giant Christmas tree in the center of the market square, and the garlands arching over the street on King. Apparently, we're avoiding any personal content, and I'm okay with that.

He insists on paying for our coffees and it's a silly detail, but I like that he gets a white chocolate mocha instead of something spare and disciplined like an Americano or a black coffee.

"Glad to see your seasonal favorite hasn't changed," he says, elbow nudging my arm gently as we wait for the walk sign.

"I can't imagine a world where I don't want peppermint mochas at Christmastime. It's so perfect." I sip, savoring the rich, minty-sweet flavor of what is mostly sugary syrup with a touch of espresso.

When I open my eyes, he's watching. Not staring at my lips or leaning in to kiss me—he's just watching. And there's this softness in his gaze that makes my heart twist.

The walk sign chirps and we move on reflex, quiet until we get to the other side. Old Town Books is just down the street and I love that this is the plan. He's always been a reader—or he used to be. So have I. Our lives were nothing alike as kids, but we both loved books. Mine may have been bought and paid for brand-new and his came from the library, but we had that in common from the very start.

"There's a special holiday event. It's a bookmark-making thing? I got us tickets, but we don't have to do it."

The twinge of nervousness in his words has me acting without thought. I simply grab his hand, ignore the ensuing butterflies, and pull him into the store.

Half an hour later, we've each crafted little bookmarks that look like Santa and his reindeer threw up on them. Red glitter and bright green pompoms and sparkling gold sequins on the tassels.

"Well, this is hideous." He holds his up, and a section with too much glue oozes down the face a quarter-inch.

I cup his warm hand and twist it so he's holding the mark flat. "Hey! Don't ruin that masterpiece. An angel loses its halo every time a tacky Christmas craft is maligned."

We chuckle together, grinning and delighting in each other. Our linked hands are peppered with little squares of red and green glitter despite having washed them. They're cheery and kind of magical, even though they'll be plaguing us for days, no doubt.

The moment is so simple and light, so natural, that as soon as I recognize it, my hand drops away from his and I sober.

"Did you want to look at some books? Browse a little?"

I'm not sure if he senses the shift in my thoughts, or if he's simply asking, but I nod because of course I do. We head right to romance for me, and I select a few seasonal finds, then we wander over to the history section for him.

"Speaking of history, I think we should discuss *our* history. So we know how to answer anyone who asks why we've been apart." I don't want to bring us back to this reality, but we have to. I don't want to be unprepared.

His throat bobs and his gaze stays on the book he's holding for a beat. "In the meeting I had, I mentioned you stayed stateside so you could focus on your business. I think that works well enough. Plenty of spouses are geographically separated for education or work or whatever."

I nod. "Sure. Makes sense."

And it does. I can't judge how anyone else is living their life.

I happen to know that if I had this man as my husband for good, if I had him for real, nothing would keep me from being as close to him as I could get.

That's where the shine of the flecks of glitter still on my fingers wears off, I guess. Because I won't have him that way. Not ever.

CHAPTER FOURTEEN

Janie

Colin and I have swapped a handful of texts each day, but that's it. He asked to bring me lunch, then to take me to dinner, but I've put him off. Being with him at the bookstore, making our crafts, laughing together, it was too much. Too good.

I can't let this door open any wider—it won't be simple to shut it again and I can't risk that. Not now. Not with him. Not again.

I'm nearly seasick at the thought of being close to him tonight and I've worked my way through as many of the messy feelings trying to crush me as I can. But after our Christmassy little adventure on Sunday, I needed space.

I needed to remember I have a full life without him. So yes, being near him can make it hard to breathe for how much I wish things were different between us, but that's not a new feeling.

My work is satisfying, if currently frustrating thanks to some of my clients—looking at you, Isabella! My friends are wonderful. My family is a challenge. But my cousin and Andy are delightful, and we've gotten even closer in the last year, which I love. It's all good and full and meaningful.

And I don't need him to embrace it.

So this plan will do a few specific jobs. I'll spend time with my old friend, scare away my would-be "suitor"—a far too generous word for Barron—and try to enjoy the holidays while not feeling too empty inside about the whole situation.

Because I'm not empty. I'm full.

Almost too full.

Practically brimming!

Based on the way my pulse is racing as the time ticks down to when I need to leave to meet Colin, I'm unlikely to maintain my sanity quite so smoothly as I'm pretending I will. But I have no choice. This is a "fake it till you make it" situation and that's all there is to say about it.

When Colin said he had a casual work event *tonight*, just a few days after agreeing to stay married and show up for him as his wife, I said I'd be there. But as I check the corners of my cat-eye liner and straighten my deep red dress that looks like it could be worn for an upscale business meeting until I paired it with black patent heels, more dramatic makeup, and a pristine wool jacket, I'm nervous.

Like, really, really nervous.

Like, I've been walking around with kitchen towels stuffed into my armpits so I don't end up with sweat rings on the fabric under my arms right as Colin arrives.

Basically, I am all that is delicate and low maintenance and "whoopsies, I just woke up like this!"

I roll my eyes at the thought as I gather lip gloss and

some mints into my clutch, all the while willing my heart to calm down or we'll never make it out of the house alive.

The doorbell rings and my heart stops for a beat, then kicks into high gear. I stop at the mirror in my entryway and give myself a wide-eyed glare. "Get it together!" Then I strip the towels from my dress and fling them down the hallway like a madwoman covering up a murder, the ball of fabric flying far and fast enough it narrowly misses a framed photograph on the wall.

Then I'm swinging the door open to find Colin standing tall and dark and handsome on my doorstep.

Air rushes out of me and the thought I cannot avoid flashes through my mind. *I shouldn't have said yes to this.*

It's too much. The pile of longing that has built up and then been buried and paved over in my heart burst through around the time I saw him with that grumpy orange cat and I'm not sure I'll survive an evening all dressed up pretending to be his wife.

Not pretending. Simply acting like it isn't new.

His eyes slide over me and I swear they smolder when he meets my gaze, then leans in for a kiss on the cheek. "You look beautiful."

"You do, too. I—I haven't seen you in your formal uniform since..." *Since we got married in Vegas.*

It's a silly thing to say because of course I haven't seen him in uniform—I haven't seen him, period. Still, the words tumble out right along with a flush of nerves.

"I regret that's the case."

It takes my muddled mind a few minutes before I fully compute it, which is probably why I say, "You do?"

His eyes are on mine, reading every single thing I'm not sure how to say. *Why do you regret it? What does that mean?*

Why do you keep leaving me?

I hate how those thoughts come through so loud and clear, but I remind myself he can't actually read my mind. *Thank goodness.*

But those eyes... How many times have I dreamt about them? And here they are, locked into mine, and I don't want to look away. For once in this new era between us, I don't want to shy away or shrink what feels insurmountable to me.

I want to make him answer, or wait for *him* to look away. He's the one who's been leaving, who has found it so easy to walk away.

Maybe if he says it to my face, I'll get it. Maybe it'll finally penetrate my brain.

His brow wrinkles and he takes a small breath, his hand moving toward me and sliding to my waist.

My heart thrums and my lips part.

But it's he who speaks, low and gritty.

"I always regret not being near you."

This truly short-circuits my brain, not surprisingly, thrusting me back to the memory of his words in Vegas. *"What if I said I regret every second I spent without you?"*

Wouldn't it be nice if those pretty words were true?

Before I can respond in any way other than blinking, he steps back and gestures for me to move past him.

"Ready?"

I move, still in a bit of a trance, then stop in the middle of the sidewalk when I realize I have no idea where we're going. He comes alongside me, ushering us toward a nondescript gray sedan. It's so completely average, I'm smiling as he opens my door and I recall the one time I found myself getting dumped into the passenger's side of a shiny black Range Rover. When Barron slid into the driver's seat, he winked at me and said, "Hot, right?"

Hard to express how *not* hot the scenario was, let alone the gala dinner we attended thanks to my parents' pressure. It's a scenario I never wish to repeat, but more than that, it reminds me how unpretentious Colin is and always has been.

"What do I need to know about tonight?"

I only know it's a work event, nothing more. We talked about our history at the bookstore, but not much about anything else. That line of conversation effectively shut down the ease between us and not twenty minutes later, I was home, door closed behind me, all the warmth and laughter and good feelings churned up between us flattened by the harsh dose of reality.

But in the here and now, he drives us onto a main road. I like the way his hands are confident on the wheel, steering with one and shifting gears smoothly with the other. The fact that he has a manual is oddly appealing, too.

Okay, so basically everything about him is doing it for you?

Yes, self. Yes. Which is not ideal as we ease onto I-95 toward the city to spend an evening together as man and wife.

"It's an evening with the senior leadership. We need to stay at least an hour, I'd say." He shifts as he merges, driving capably but not in a showy way.

"Run me through your coworkers so far so I have at least an idea of who's who."

I don't expect to know everyone off the bat, but I'll have an easier time engaging if I can anticipate some of the names. I should've spent some time reviewing military ranks at the very least, but I didn't even think of it until right now.

He names off a handful of people, none of whom he's

known for long except a guy named Josh Coleridge whom I can tell he knows better than the rest.

"You knew Josh before being here?" I'm instantly excited to meet someone who knows him from his military life longer than the few weeks he's been in town.

"We've crossed paths at a few duty stations, but he was an Academy grad, too, so I've known him since then. He's a close friend."

His brows pinch in the middle and I have no prayer of reading his expression, so I dig a little.

"Are you worried about him meeting me? Does he know about us?" That seems like the simplest way to put it.

"He knows what happened in Vegas," he says, jaw clenching for a moment while he takes a breath, gaze still glued to the road. "But he doesn't know we're still married. I haven't seen him since I got here because I was in the in-processing course and, yeah. Could be interesting to see how he does with this."

"Are you worried?"

He exhales a big breath. "I wish I'd had a chance to give him a heads-up. I have a feeling he'll do okay with it, though."

"Maybe you can pull him aside right when we get there or something. Give the word and I'll make a distraction." I throw my hands up and wiggle my fingers as an example of a possible distraction. I need it for myself or my heart will get too heavy tonight.

He glances over, then returns to his Very Responsible Driving and shakes his head. "Yes, an unsolicited set of jazz hands will throw the leadership team for a loop."

I giggle because Colin Vicente saying "jazz hands" cracks me up, as does the idea that any amount of hand waving would do anything to a room full of war-hardened military personnel.

That thought brings a whoosh of nerves and I slump back in the seat. "I probably should've studied up a little for this. I once asked my cousin if there was anything I should know, but he claims unless it's a military ball, there's not much to know."

I attended a ball with him two years back and it was lovely, but there were protocols I haven't retained.

"He's right. And before our ball, I'll make sure to give you the rundown."

Our ball. He means his unit, his coworkers, whatever. Not us. Not... us.

"Sounds reasonable," I say, but my fingers are knitting together in my lap.

His warm, large hand reaches out and settles over my anxious movements, effectively stilling them. He's stopped at a light and looks at me straight in the eye.

"You're wonderful, CP, and they're going to love you. If by some bizarre chance they think you're anything less than completely charming, I can promise you it's their problem."

A car honks and he removes his hand, shifting gears and taking off. I'm left with tingling hands and a fluttering heart and a desperate hope that this night won't end with me in over my head.

CHAPTER FIFTEEN

Colin

The small moments of contact with Janie in the last half hour are going to be responsible for my untimely demise.

I had no illusions about how I'd feel tonight with her. There would be no way to resist feeling the pull toward her I'd experienced from the very minute I first saw her over twenty-five years ago, but I also anticipated the context of being at a work social event would quell some of the... thirst.

False.

Lies.

Utter foolishness.

Because Janie in a setting like this is almost as good as Janie with cats. She's pure charm and magnetism, her smile unstoppable and her social graces so engrained she's unfazed by even the surliest of sergeant majors.

That said, Sergeant Major Smith is currently practically

fawning over her, he and his wife giggling at an anecdote Janie's sharing. The man has given only the sparest hint of acknowledgement he is human in the few encounters I've had with him, and yet here he is smiling full-out, snuggling his wife into his side like Janie's brightness is fueling a new level of affection for his beloved and all mankind.

It's stunning and yet not at all a surprise.

A messy spill of old feelings I don't like to acknowledge stirs in my gut. I hate that it sneaks in like this, but seeing her charm the room, I can't deny it's her pedigree. The way she was raised and the reality that she's always just been *better*.

Cringing away from the thought, I focus on her. On now. Because those old thought patterns aren't worth lingering on. They aren't real.

"Colin, how did you two meet?" Mrs. Gleeson, the unit commander's wife, asks with a beaming smile.

"We met when we were kids. Our houses were a few blocks from each other and I wrecked my bike in her yard. She patched me up, then proceeded to boss me around for the next twenty-plus years." It's not far from the truth, though it's a little simplistic.

Everyone chuckles but Janie's shaking her head at me, lips pursed. "Boss you around, huh? I seem to remember you being extremely stubborn."

I shrug, enjoying this small trip down memory lane. "Now, now, CP. Just accept that you were a little boss."

"CP?" Mrs. Gleeson interjects, and everyone's brows raise as though this question is burning through them equally.

Janie's face flames with a gorgeous blush, and I snake an arm around her waist, pulling her to me.

"When we met, this one was obsessed with Cabbage

Patch dolls. She bossed them around in the absence of actual human playmates." I can feel her rolling her eyes next to me, her head shake attempting to counter my words. I turn to face her, my gaze cataloguing those features I've been taken by all my life—dark blue eyes, perfect nose, soft lips. "Actually, I always liked how she took care of them. She was so gentle with them, even though they were dolls. And she had this big imagination long after most kids lost theirs."

Our gazes connect, her eyes glittering back at me, emotions brimming.

What I'm not saying is that the first time I called her this nickname, it was to stop her crying. She turned ten and her dad threw away all her dolls—not gave them away, but threw them away. He told her she was too old for toys, and she was devastated. She hadn't played with them much, but she'd been gutted that those old friends wouldn't find a second home, find someone else to love them. Even at twelve, I'd recognized it wasn't childishness that had her sobbing. It was her softness, her stalwart way of caring for things without limits.

So I'd called her Cabbage Patch as a joke, an effort to distract her, and it stuck.

"That's adorable," Mrs. Gleeson coos, right as Mrs. Smith chimes, "You two are precious."

"That is just *so* precious, truly. How long have you two been married?"

My head snaps to the left to see Josh standing there, a jaunty smirk on his face, but suspicion in his eyes. He's arriving fashionably late and therefore I had no opportunity to tell him what's going on.

Janie grins, her social mask unmoved by the question. "We just celebrated our five-year anniversary."

"Have you? How nice," Josh says, then pins me with a look that says "prepare to explain yourself."

"And you all? How long have you been married and living this amazing military life?"

Janie's pivot away from us is welcome and expert. The two couples attending her answer, but I press a kiss to her cheek which makes her lashes flutter, then whisper, "Be right back."

Her eyes catch mine and since we talked about me taking a moment for him, I can tell she understands I've got to deal with Smirks McGee over here before he has a hissy fit.

He's already walking to the bar, knowing I'll follow, and we circle up as the bartender pours him a drink and takes my order.

"So you're married. Five years now, huh?"

The tone isn't mad, but it's demanding, and I rush to fill in the gaps.

"Long story short? My mom never submitted the final dissolution paperwork and we stayed married." I duck my head and speak as quietly as I can. "I found out when I did my security interview and they asked about my wife."

His eyes widen and he huffs a disbelieving laugh. "Well, shoot, man. That's sticky."

I accept the beer and champagne from the bartender after dropping a tip in the bowl. "Yeah. Just a bit. And the fact that she's here playing along so I don't look like a security risk is a miracle."

He snorts a laugh into his beer. After drinking a sip, he pins me with a glare. "Weird that the woman you've been obsessed with since you were seven but keep running away from would be a touch hesitant to play wife after you married her then ditched her with little more than a goodbye five years ago."

"Well, I guess you're familiar with at least part of our history," Janie says.

Josh and I turn slowly to find her standing behind us, a strained smile on her face.

Dread settles over me because she clearly heard every word of Josh's comment. Every bit of it. So she knows I told him how I left her after Vegas, how I haven't been in touch. And she heard the beginning part, too, which is embarrassing enough.

I panic a bit, wanting to cover up the awkwardness stretching between us and redirect the conversation, so I jump in. "Janie, hey—"

"Janie, love, it's nice to finally meet the woman this guy's been talking about since the day I met him."

CHAPTER SIXTEEN

Janie

Josh's honesty is refreshing and, if I'm honest, a little thrilling.

I'll admit, I can't help but enjoy the embarrassed flush of Colin's cheeks nor the sneaky twinkle in his best friend's eye.

"It's nice to meet you, too. I've heard very little about you, sadly, but I'm guessing you're not surprised by that."

Josh's dark brows tilt in a troubled frown and he pouts at Colin for a minute before winking at me.

"I am not the least bit surprised. If ever there was a man who is both unendingly generous and yet somehow extremely miserly with personal information, it's him." He nudges Colin with an elbow.

Colin startles, almost like he'd been lost in his own little world while we talked about him, then extends a hand holding a champagne flute.

"Drink?"

His eyes meet mine and I can't read them, but I take it from him gladly. "Thank you."

I want to ask how he knew I'd like champagne, but it's not a huge surprise. The bar selection is limited since we're in an event space attached to some other, larger government space. Frankly, I'm surprised there's any alcohol, but I'm not mad about having something in hand.

"So how's this going to work?" Josh asks, one brow raised.

Colin's eyes shoot to mine. "We'll be attending a few events together. And then..."

"And then we'll go our separate ways. Just like we've always done." Even though it'll be totally weird because we'll finally be living in the same place again.

It hurt when he shut me out in the past, but there was a small part of me that allowed for it to make sense. I excused it because hey, we lived miles apart, and maybe it was easier on him. The military academy isn't easy—Will reminded me of that after Colin first left. Colin was doing the hard thing by being gone, then by serving the country, by facing deployments and trainings and living in barracks. Whatever he needed to do to survive it, to thrive in that setting, he should do, or so I thought.

So I begged myself to believe.

Over the years, it has been harder to stomach that explanation, especially as he's risen in rank and the hardship of the life he chose seems less obvious. But that's me, focusing on me, and not accounting for what it's like to be at the whims of the military. How would I know?

I do know the thought of going radio silent yet again fills me with dread and a preemptive regret for getting involved in any of this. That's exactly why I'll be the one to make sure I *know* we won't be communicating after we're done here.

"Oh, yeah? Just like that—just like you've always done, huh?" Josh's skepticism is clear, and it's not misplaced.

If Colin isn't worried about it, good for him. I'm not letting on that I am, though.

"We've been apart for most of our lives at this point. Why would we do anything else?" I toss this out like it's obvious to everyone even though it makes my heart sink.

Colin clears his throat but doesn't speak.

Josh waits a beat before he says, "Right. Well. I'll look forward to seeing how that goes, then."

Someone calls his name and he excuses himself, leaving me and Colin to face each other without a buffer.

"I think we can probably leave soon. We've stayed our hour." He takes another sip of his beer, then sets it aside half-empty.

"Whatever you think. I've enjoyed meeting your coworkers." I chuckle at how odd that sounds. "I guess they're more than coworkers? Or, is that what people say for military stuff?"

"Coworkers fits. It can feel different, especially when deployed because you see each other twenty-four-seven, but that's what they are." He glances over toward where Josh is talking with Colonel Gleeson and his wife, the chiseled cut of Colin's smooth jaw and long line of his neck scrambling my brain for a moment before I realize he's clenching his teeth.

"You okay?" I set a hand on his arm, wanting to comfort him.

"Yes. I mean, yeah. I—" He shakes his head, the first sign of true discomfort or worry I've seen from him tonight. "I can't mess this up. This next year is critical for my career, and if they suspect there's anything off here, it could look bad. Of course, in theory, it shouldn't reflect on anything professional, but the lines get blurry."

"That's why I'm here, right? To make sure they see we're a real couple, that nothing is amiss. They don't know we didn't interact for the last five years, and we don't ever have to discuss that, right? I mean, is there some kind of lie detector test you have to take?"

He chuckles and looks at me with a softness I miss more than I should.

"No. No lie detector. But I don't like lying." He shakes his head, jaw flexing. "I'm sorry about this."

I take his hand in mine and wait for him to give me his eyes. When he does, I squeeze for emphasis. "We'll be fine, and you'll be fine. From what I've heard, you've already made a good impression. I have no idea if you're good at your job or not, but seems like you probably are. So do a good job and relax knowing this curveball is one we're catching together."

His gaze drops to his feet, but he weaves our fingers together, then smiles up at me. "Baseball metaphors, huh? That's a quality pep talk, CP."

This comment reminds me, and I shove him with my free hand. "By the way, what the heck was with saying I was *obsessed* with Cabbage Patch dolls?"

But when I say the words, I hear Josh's voice saying *the woman you've been obsessed with since you were seven* and I nearly choke on the memory.

My words must not conjure the same recollection for him, because he just pulls me close again and raises my hand, letting it hover just below his mouth as he stares into my eyes with his endless ones.

My stomach flips as a slow smile pulls one side of his

mouth up, up, until his eyes are sparkling. He drops a kiss to my hand, slow and wildly erotic despite it being a kiss on the back of my hand, then releases me and simply says, "Because you were."

I laugh, breaking the spell, and he joins me, but then he takes my arm and tucks it in his. "Let's get out of here, wife."

"Sounds good, husband." I manage a chuckle that sounds lighthearted and not a little sad.

Because I'm not sad. I've had a nice time. I've done what I said I'd do.

And if I'm falling further under Colin Vicente's spell— something I've never needed any help with—then I guess so be it.

CHAPTER SEVENTEEN

Colin

My sister bangs on the door and doesn't stop until I answer it, foggy-headed from lack of sleep and over-socialization last night.

With one hand on her hip and heaps of judgement in her eyes, she only says, "Really?" and barges past me.

I don't need to ask what she's talking about. There's only one way she would've found out what's going on, and clearly, she's not impressed.

"Mom told you." I follow her into the living room, still boring white with only a couch, coffee table, and TV to speak of.

She whips around to face me and the dead-eyed glare would be enough to cow another man—someone who hadn't grown up with her dramatics.

"Yes. Our mother told me you got married to Janie *five years ago*—didn't tell me, in case anyone's keeping track—

then proceeded to *stay* married to her and now you're using her so you don't get fired because you know the military will think it's sketchy as all get-out and she gets nothing from the whole arrangement." She crosses her arms, her glare somehow intensifying. "Yeah. She told me."

I take a breath, remembering I have been under much worse stress and I kept it together. But my little sister accusing me of using Janie doesn't sit right.

Maybe because you are.

"Did Mom happen to mention it was her shenanigans that meant we didn't end up divorced?"

She raises a single, judgmental brow. "Yes. And all that told me was that you were using your run-and-hide plan like you always do with her."

Her means Janie, not our mother.

Bianca and Lina always loved Janie and her brother Chip. And worse, they knew *I* loved her.

"Listen, I'm not trying to use her. Or—" I run a hand through my hair and let out a pent-up breath. "She's aware. She knows the deal. And she's getting something out of this, too. So it's working for both of us."

Lina nods rapidly, lashes fluttering. "Mmkay, mmkay, mmkay, and what about how you're still in love with her? What about that?"

I laugh. "I'm not."

She stares.

"Lina, I'm really not. I'll admit I used to be, but I don't even know her anymore."

But everything I learn, I like. Everything I remember is still there. Every part of her is becoming more beautiful.

There's also the voice shouting at me saying I do know her. Our time together last night proved it—we clicked. We were convincing to everyone and we've hardly spent a handful of hours together since Vegas. That's because *I know her.*

Lina gives a long, steading exhale. Her expression shifts as she looks around, evidently taking in my place for the first time. "I'm sorry, but are you secretly a serial killer? What is with the creepy monochrome? Not even a little tree or something?"

An exhausted chuckle trips out. "Not a serial killer, no. My stuff is still on a ship somewhere in the Atlantic and I haven't had much downtime since getting back." And maybe it feels a touch meaningless to decorate a house that feels more like a landing pad than a home.

She scowls. "Listen, I—"

"Knock, knock, Vicente. Your door was open so I'm hoping you weren't burgled."

Josh's voice reaches us right before he saunters into view. Lina halts her speech and sucks in a shocked breath.

"Please, do come in," I say waving him in even as he walks right into the living room and pulls Lina into a hug.

A small *ooph* slips out of her as he squeezes her, then releases and looks down. He's grinning, wide-eyed as he says, "Little Vicente!"

But then his gaze drops down over her, and his face follows—the smirky smile he always shot my siblings melting into something entirely different.

Idiot Stunned, if the sculpture had a name.

He hasn't seen either of my sisters in years, and Lina has grown up considerably since. He probably realizes he shouldn't have snatched her up into a hug like she's a child, but serves him right for being here at all.

"Hey, Josh." Lina's expression shutters in a flash, and she grins. "I see you're here to berate this candy cane-for-brains, too?"

Josh is still moving slowly because it takes him a beat before he piles on. When he does, he clears his throat, spearing a hand through his hair, and winks at her, charm recovered. "You know it. I witnessed the couple in real life last night and let me say..." He shakes his hand like he touched something hot.

Lina's hands slap together and she clasps them in front of her mouth as though she's containing her excitement.

And so she was, because it erupts.

"You have to finally admit you've been in love with her forever! You're still married and it's not by chance. Just give in and be happy for once in your life, please!" A touch of sisterly whining twinges the end.

Josh grins over at her, then claps his hands together in the same supplicating gesture. "Yes, please. Be happy, for Christmas's sake!"

I remain unmoved. Their pleas fall on deaf ears.

Because it's not up to me.

It's not that I'm not tempted, but it's not just up to me.

And it's not like it would work, anyway.

Josh snaps and points, his signature gesture. "That. What is that look? Tell me right now, no hedging, no nonsense. *Tell me.*"

For a guy who can present a charming façade, underneath it, he's a bossy jerk sometimes. Exhibit A is right now.

"I'm not—"

Lina groans, eyes shooting to plead with the heavens, and Josh scowls at me, intensity building as though the harder he stares, the more honest I'll be.

And for some reason, the twin assault from them, two people who've known me so much of my life, unlocks the words.

"I've never been good enough for her, and nothing's

changed. I won't fit in her life, and she—" I start to say she won't fit in mine, but it's a lie. She fit seamlessly last night. She made everything better and easier, like always. So it's not that she won't fit, but rather I fear and say aloud, "She won't want any part of this life."

Josh's eyes narrow, inspecting me, while Lina presses a hand against her heart.

"If she's too stupid to see how unique the military life is, that's her problem. I know I don't totally get it as just your sister, but I'm so proud of you, and I'd be honored to be with someone who serves." Her gaze cuts to the left where Josh's jaw has hardened, but he's still staring at me, then she adds, "She's a fool if she wouldn't consider you because you're in the Army."

I absorb that, guilt flooding in because I know I've created this fiction and it's all nonsense. It's unfair to her. She never shied away from this part of my life.

It was always up to me. Always me distancing myself for my own sake, to keep the crushing longing at bay and avoid the utter agony of wanting something I knew I couldn't have for any longer than I already had it. *Her.*

Worked like a charm, huh?

Josh folds his arms and he won't stop staring at me, so finally I widen my eyes and give him a "what?" look.

He tsks. "I know I'm your best friend and I'm supposed to be super supportive and all, but I'm going to have to call BS on this whole situation."

I straighten, bracing. He has the look that tells me whatever is next is going to be ugly.

"Yeah, because I saw you last night. You weren't your usual awkward, dreading small talk self. You were happy. And I realize I just met her last night, but she seemed happy, too."

A rough chuckle trips out of me. "Well, she's amazing in social situations. She'd never let on if she was anything else. You never would've known."

He does the annoying tsk again. "Sure, sure. Let's say that's true. I still think she liked being there, and she loved being there with you. More than that, though..." His jaw flexes, and I suck in a breath.

His gaze is hard when he speaks. "I don't want to hear you say you're not good enough. Not again."

Internally, I wince, but externally, I shake my head. "Sadly, you don't get to choose."

Lina's rapt, watching every twitch or blink between us, practically shoveling popcorn into her mouth like a live-action meme. Josh continues as though I haven't spoken.

"She comes from a rich family. So what? Income disparity doesn't indicate the value of a human being."

I grumble because of course, logically, I know he's right. I've always known this on some level, and the Gruff family's insistence on being people who accentuate the difference rather than minimize it bothered me. It was only Janie who didn't seem to care I came from a few blocks away and in a sense, a world apart from hers.

"Is it because of Dad?"

Lina's question breaks through my thoughts and clearly surprises Josh, based on the breath he sucks in.

The thing is, we don't talk about our dad. I've mentioned him once or twice to Josh over our nearly fifteen-year friendship. He's certainly not going to comment now, but it's the smallness, that edge of pain, that makes me speak up.

"I'll admit it doesn't help my curb appeal to have a felon for a father."

Lina's gaze casts to the ground and she nods in commiseration, but all it does is make me sick. A pinch in my jaw, my mouth waters like I could empty my stomach just thinking about the garbage choices my father made and how they're still, decades later, affecting his kids.

I rush to her and take her shoulders in my hands.

"Hey, just because he's a jackass doesn't mean we've got the stink of his mistakes on us, right? We're our own people, and same goes for Bianca and her kids and Mom. What he did isn't our story."

Her head slowly raises until she hits me with her blue gaze and I finally register the gleam in them as she smirks.

"Exactly. So buck up, stop making excuses, and stay married to my sister-in-law."

CHAPTER EIGHTEEN

Janie

Fidgeting is one of my many sins—just ask my mother. How many times did she tell me to *just sit still* as a kid? And how many times did her hand clamp down on mine in an effort to keep me from twisting my fingers together?

Countless. Especially since so much of my childhood featured fancy parties and work events for my parents, plus the occasional excitement brought by my uncle's time serving as a US senator, there were ample opportunities for my mother to find my manners lacking.

To be fair, they could be. But boys didn't have to cross their legs at the ankle. For that matter, they didn't have to wear horrible tights under dresses or have their hair pulled back into ponytails so tight they changed the shape of their forehead. At least when we got Angela, our second house-keeper, the hairstyles got better.

"Hey, sorry I'm late."

Colin's deep voice pulls me from my memory lane walk and I rise to greet him, pressing a kiss to the air at the side of his face in a gesture so automatic and empty, it's startling.

Literally, I stop, shake my head, and say, "Wait, let me do that again."

Because I'm not greeting some friend or acquaintance. In this context, surrounded by people who could know me or my husband, I want to make sure it's clear we are more.

A chuckle slips out and he leans in for a half hug, but I pull him close, letting our bodies press against one another from knees to shoulders as I wrap my arms around his neck and imprint a slow, purposeful kiss to his cheek.

Yes, it may be because one of Chip's old flames is in the room and I know she tends to be chatty with my family and Barron's. I don't want word on the street to be that I met an acquaintance or someone who could be a long-time business associate. I want it known I met someone significant.

Also, I need a hug, and Colin's great at them. Always has been. Forgive me if I coerced it a bit.

Instead of letting my little squeeze and peck be it, Colin's arms wrap around my torso and his face tucks low into my neck. He inhales slowly and the brush of his mouth and nose plus the slight scrape of what stubble has muscled its way back even from this morning sends a shiver through me.

We both take a breath, here in the middle of a crowded district lunch spot, before breaking apart.

"Thanks, I needed that," he says, his gaze so soft on me, my stomach somersaults.

"Likewise."

"You looked like you were pretty deep in thought. Everything okay?"

We settle into the two-person seat at a classic DC lunch spot, Old Ebbitt Grill. It's historic and the Victorian-American style interior has a lush quality I've always enjoyed. The booths feature velvet-cushioned backs, the wood is all dark and polished to a high shine, and murals grace the walls depicting the Capitol building, White House, and various people and scenes from the area or its history. The restaurant, with historical roots as a boarding house and saloon, is often full of people wanting to be seen. Today, we're here because it's not far from where Colin works, and I'm craving pie.

I run a hand over the pristine white tablecloth, appreciating the bright pops among all the dark wood. It's a smart move to use the cloths despite the fact that the fare here isn't particularly elevated. It's good, if expensive, but we aren't talking about fine dining. It all works together to create the feeling of opulence and history, and I like that.

But I'm also stalling, wondering how honest to be while I admire the crown molding. Our night at his work event ended without any remarkable issues. We left the party on good terms, he took me home and I tried not to ogle his hands and wrists as he drove, and then I kissed his cheek, slipped out of the car, and practically sprinted to my door to avoid a doorstep moment.

Because I'm a chicken.

I admit it.

But the earlier thoughts remembering my parents, and maybe even being in *this* place, a location in which I've definitely been reprimanded more than once over the years, has me feeling oddly raw.

"I was thinking about how it used to drive my mom crazy that I couldn't sit still."

He laughs softly, then takes a sip of the ice water

already on the table before responding. "Yeah, I always wondered why she'd correct you, but somehow never seemed bothered that Chip couldn't stay still, let alone even stay in his seat."

I smile at a flash of memories—Chip exploring the restaurant, Chip sneaking off to play outside, Chip abandoning all pretense of paying attention to whatever was happening and often disappearing entirely.

"He got away with so much," I agree, shaking my head at the memory. It doesn't hurt the way it used to. I had such a tender spot about that for years, and admittedly, I can feel the ache at times. But Chip and I are closer now than we've ever been, and this has come through determination on both of our parts to heal.

I always saw Chip as the blessed golden child who could do no wrong even though he often did actually make stupid mistakes. I saw all manner of idiotic choices being waved away because he was the first-born son and cooperated with what they wanted him to do—fencing and tennis, attending Princeton, then transitioning into law like a good boy.

What shocked me was how he saw me—a kid who got away with doing what she wanted despite it being outside of expectations. Instead of an Ivy League school, I dared to go to George Mason right here in town. "Not even Georgetown?" my father had asked, not so much disappointed as irritated. I'm not sure he could feel something as strong as disappointment for me.

Then came the major—a BA in Art and Visual Technology with a focus in interior design rather than anything else. They pleaded with me about this early on, then decided to ignore it. They always did have a bit of an "ignore it long enough and it'll go away" approach to parenting, and were perpetually surprised it wasn't particularly effective. Upon my graduation, they spoke about opportunities to pursue master's degrees in something "worthwhile."

Chip saw me as being free, not judged and tolerated. I saw him as privileged, not trapped and losing himself. Once we realized the truth, a lot of the sting eased.

A warm hand covers mine and I look up to find Colin waiting patiently, and a waiter staring down at me. I order quickly—the grilled chicken with winter greens and ancient grain salad and a promise to myself I'll get pie to take home —and the waiter leaves. Colin must've ordered while I was locked away in my own head.

"I'm sorry. I don't know what's going on today," I say, but then shake my head. "Or maybe it's the text from my mom saying she heard I'm refusing to be nice to Barron."

"Barron?" His eyes are wide. "She wants you to be nice to a guy named Barron?"

"Barron Banks, and yes, *obviously*."

He laughs as he takes a swallow of water and nearly chokes. Once recovered, he reaches for my hand and holds it firm. "I'm going to insist we make it very clear you're unavailable for anything *Barron Banks* wants."

I make no effort to stifle my grin. "That's something you're going to help me with, right?"

There's a look in his eyes I can't quite identify—like he's just had an idea, but I have no guess as to what.

"I'll help you with that, and more." He winks, then grins.

Flustered, I reach for my water, wondering what that means, but the waiter delivers our drinks. I feel eyes on me, and that's part of the bonus here, though I'm nervous thinking about what more my parents will have to say. But I shouldn't care.

"I'm tired of caring what they think," I finally say after a sip of the cranberry-lime mocktail I ordered. I'm not a day drinker, but I wanted something fun, and all of their seasonal drinks drew me in.

"You shouldn't, but I get it." His eyes dash away, then return to mine. "I still get wrapped up in thinking about my dad too much. I hate that I do, but whether I like it or not, he's my dad."

I remember when he found out his dad was going to jail. He wouldn't talk to me for three days, until I finally tracked him down and made him.

I was fifteen and he was seventeen. He was always cagey about his dad, and I rarely saw Mr. Vicente around—just his mom, Martha. But that day, he joked about me being a stalker when I found him, swallowed hard, and then he cried. Cried and cried, so much I got scared worrying about what had happened. Our families didn't run in the same circles, so there were no whispers like there would've been if it'd been one of my parents or their friends.

When he finally told me, I was relieved. I remember this incredible loosening in my chest because I was terrified it was something worse. And yet he was gutted, and looking back, I didn't fully understand why. Of course I knew it was bad his dad was going to jail, but I didn't get what that meant for him and his family.

And until I saw him work so hard to make a career for himself built off of tenets like integrity and discipline, I still didn't. Even now, he holds himself to a standard so high because he's attempting to make up for the ways his father failed his family.

That's why we're here. To connect, make sure we're convincingly married at the next event, and ultimately help things remain steady. I need to remember this and not get it confused, even when he's opening up a little. Even when he's making me feel seen in ways so few people can.

To keep his career, we'll keep lying.

Colin

Thinking about Janie is my new part-time job.

Granted, Josh would likely argue that's nothing new. But he can jump in a frozen lake, because I don't have time to think about the past. There's just one week left until most people take leave for Christmas. We've got the ball coming up Saturday night, then many of my peers will be gone until after New Year's.

I don't normally take much time off. It's always benefitted me to hang around and fill in the gaps, then take time later. When our personnel officer saw how much leave I've accumulated, she looked me straight in the eye and told me I had to take some because if the commander found out I'm a workaholic, he'd be disappointed.

Have I been racing to justify my existence and bury the past embarrassment and shame produced by my father's felonious proclivities? Yes. Thank you, Dr. Vanessa Santiago, for helping me with that one a few years back.

Has this realization changed anything for me? I'm not sure.

Except, for the first time I can remember, I'm not preoccupied with work. I'm not brainstorming how to make sure my commanding officer is impressed enough to give me the top block I need for my promotion packet. Instead, I'm thinking about her.

Janie.

My wife.

A shuddering thrill runs through me with the thought, but on its heels comes the knowledge I shouldn't get comfortable with such language. *That way lies dragons.*

Still, our lunch a few days ago gave me an idea that may actually be quite foolish or end in some real awkwardness and regret, but I can't shake it.

And speaking of, it's lunch time and I'm meeting Janie again. We planned on yesterday as a way to reconnect and get to know each other a bit more before we're spending several hours with coworkers at a sit-down dinner, but today's lunch is all me.

Josh hollers after me, jogging toward my car as I open the driver's side door. He's wearing a sparkly red swath of tinsel like a scarf.

"You've got the spirit going. Good work."

Fortunately, Josh's office is right down the hallway in the same building and his direct-report boss is apparently a huge Christmas fan, so everyone defiles their uniforms with various out-of-regulation décor during the last week before the holiday block leave period.

He fluffs the tinsel around his shoulders and flashes his

brows. "Thank you, Major. And where are you off to so urgently? I thought we could grab lunch."

"Ah, sorry, I'm meeting Janie."

His smile grows slowly, with great dramatic effect. "Oh, are you? A second day in a row?"

I'm not going to be late just to listen to him tease me. "Yep. I'll talk to you later."

He bows and sweeps a hand, gesturing for me to be on my way. I roll my eyes and make sure he sees it as he straightens, but he just winks, the twerp.

"Have fun with your wife!" he yells after me, like this is some kind of insult.

He thinks he's funny. He also means well. He wants me to be happy, to miraculously find that Janie and I were always meant to be together despite my perpetual mistrust that we could ever work, let alone that I'm right for her.

I turn on the Christmas music and focus on "Last Christmas," by Wham! then abruptly change it because it feels a little too on the nose if I think about our wedding years ago and then what could happen now. Only difference is, she didn't cause the tears. I did that quite effectively all by myself.

By the time I make it out of the city and to the little Mexican restaurant she recommended, Tacos Y Tacos, I've shaken off the funk Wham! foisted up on me and let Michael Bublé's dulcet classic Christmas songs ease the ache.

Janie's walking up to the door from the opposite direction, frowning down at her phone. It gives me a chance to admire the long, Christmas-red wool coat she's wearing, with black boots and something underneath that will no doubt make my mouth water.

Because I'm hungry. That's all.

When she glances up, I'm already holding the door.

"Oh, hey." She chuckles, a light blush coasting across her pretty cheeks. "Sorry, I was reading an email."

"Work drama?" I ask, using the same phrase she's used once or twice when talking about clients wanting their way against her and her team's better judgement.

"You could say that."

I follow her inside, and the host seats us at a table with cherry-red booths. Garlands crisscross the space—avocado halves wearing Santa hats, green-glittered lime wedges and margarita glasses with golden sparkling contents, and so many Santa hats and red and green accents, it's hard to know where to look.

We sit and I'm still taking it all in. "This is festive."

She grins. "I'd never eaten here until Andy and Grace brought me and I've been hooked ever since. My office relocated not far from here last year so it's walkable."

She's smiling down at the menu and my heart squeezes like the stupid little jock of a muscle it is. Like reps will make it stronger instead of proving how every second with this woman is making me weak.

Alas, when her bright eyes hit mine and she asks, "What do you want?", I only narrowly miss saying, "You."

Instead, I fumble, clearing my throat and frantically eying the options like I should've been when I was studying her and say, "Fajitas."

After ordering, she shifts into a kind of work mode I find wildly appealing because it's so direct and focused. I like every part of her I've seen, and this is just one more. She's asking about the ball this weekend, confirming the appropriate attire and timing. She's wondering if I need anything from her other than to be ready at whatever time I want to pick her up.

This is the moment, I realize, so I take it. "If you have the time, I need you to come with me after lunch, just for a few minutes. Maybe fifteen?"

"Sure, I can swing it. My meeting this afternoon is at two, so I just need to be back a few minutes before to prep." She smiles. "I'm kind of looking forward to the ball. Is that cheesy?"

Is thinking about you every second of every day cheesy?

"No, it's not. It's an interesting tradition. I never thought about how there's nothing like it in civilian life, probably because your family was always going to galas."

At least once a month, her parents were off to another fundraising gala of one kind or another, bespoke tux for her dad and some expensive, fancy dress for her mom. I'd catch glimpses of them occasionally, right before they left and I snuck in to hang with Janie without her parents there to interrupt.

And no. We never got into any trouble they wouldn't have approved of because I never once made a move.

I had chances. There were opportunities, a few I can recall with a tightening stomach, but our food arrives and brings me back to the moment.

She chats about her clients, dropping mention of how her parents are ready for her to "quit her little hobby."

"Your *hobby*? You have a business. Don't you have, like, four employees?"

She tilts her head side to side, chewing a bite of her chimichanga. Once she swallows, she elaborates. "Two full-time, two-part time. But I've been in business for almost eight years now. They hardly recognized it in the first few years, then they started sending friends my way and I swear it's the worst, most difficult people. I'm doing huge renovations for their friends and they somehow still think it's this piddly little hobby." She laughs mirthlessly. "I guess in the context of their experience, it sort of is."

"No, don't let them off the hook. There's no reason for them to treat your business, something you built with hard work and determination, like this even if they don't personally see the value in it. That's not the barometer for your success and it's deeply sad for them."

She smiles softly. "Thank you. And yes, I know."

After a few more bites, she dives back into other design talk, then asks about how I'm liking my new job, office, life in the US. I'm antsy for what comes next, but I stay in the moment the best I can, until it's time to go.

We roll out of Tacos Y Tacos and stroll down the street a few blocks until we arrive. When I reach for the door, Janie gives me a perplexed look.

"Are we getting coffee?" She glances up at the Andy's Place sign.

I've been thinking about doing this for years, honestly, and yesterday's conversation about her parents and Chip and all of that clinched it. Today's only furthered the resolve, and since I've got everything set up, it's time.

She's waited too long for this. She deserves something good for herself that *she* wants, and I'm going to be the one to give it to her, if she'll let me. She deserves every good thing and if this is a starting place, well...

I grin. "We can if you want. I'm giving you your Christmas present."

CHAPTER TWENTY

Janie

I'm not certain what's happening, but I think I know.

Especially when I enter the café portion and find Andy beaming so wide the smile nearly eats her face, and Will is standing next to her. Well, Will standing next to her at any given time is nothing new. But he's got a smile twitching at his lips, which is practically a banner unfurling above their heads.

"Why, hello there, Cousin," I say to Will, then widen my eyes at Andy before returning back to him. "You might remember Colin Vicente? He was—"

"Your best friend for years? I do seem to recall." Will steps around Andy with a hand on her hip and extends the opposite to Colin, who takes it. "Good to see you."

They exchange brief military-speak discussing the unit Colin's in and where I think Will's preparing to retire from. They swap graduation class years since they're both USMA graduates, and all the while Andy is nearly bursting out of her skin.

The barista on duty shoos the whole group and Andy says, "We'll meet you upstairs," leaving me and Colin at the door to the Cat Zone.

"So..." I say, hoping he'll fill in the blanks.

"So, I'd like to buy you a cat for Christmas." He holds his hands up like I might protest, but I have no intention of doing so.

I'm too surprised, but I'm also instantly on board. It's like being on a rollercoaster, one bringing the best kind of thrills, not fear.

"I know you've held off for years, so if you really don't feel right about it, of course I don't want to pressure you. But after hearing you talk about your folks and walking through all of that yesterday, I can't help but feel like it might be time for you to do this. And I'd love to do it with you."

I am weirdly emotional. I swallow reflexively, and then I do it again, but I'm practically choking on *feelings*. It's so sweet and thoughtful. It's meaningful. I'm excited, and somehow him suggesting it feels like the permission I haven't been able to give myself. I probably need to unpack why that is, but for now, I want to ride this wave of goodness right up the stairs and find my kitty baby.

"I'd love to."

"Now, I already know who I'm getting, but you'll want to shop around and see who fits, I'm sure. So if now isn't enough time, then we'll come back another time. I've already asked Andy if we can wait until Sunday to come get them so you have some time to settle in without work and such."

I could swear he said he didn't think he could have a cat

and I wanted to ask what changed, but I'm speechless and my heart is bursting. He's thought through so much. I mentioned how I'm taking ten days off starting Monday. I'm actually a little nervous about it—about how I'll fill the time, even though I'll still be working a little from home. I need a break, and I want to feel like I've reset before the new year. Having a new little kitty buddy would be perfect.

But also... "Wait, who are you getting?"

He opens the door and gives me a funny look. "Goob, of course. I thought I couldn't have a cat, but I knew the minute I saw him that cat was meant for me."

And that's when I realize I am well and truly doomed with this man.

After wandering the space and checking in with every cat, the answer is clear. The one little love I'd spotted the first time we came but didn't get to snuggle is still here, and it just so happens he was curled up like yin to Goob's yang when we first arrived.

Goob has found his way into Colin's arms again and is fully at peace there. He looks like he might nod off, and Colin appears to feel completely settled. But it's the tiny, mottled shorthair with a white belly and boots and brown and black swirls on his back and head I can't stop smiling at who has me.

"His name is Snickerdoodle. Best we can tell, he's three," Andy says, an adoring expression on her face as she watches me pet the little fellow.

"He's so small, I thought maybe he wasn't fully

grown," I marvel, running the pad of my finger over the soft, short fur at his forehead. I kind of love his name, too. So many possible nicknames are already springing to mind.

"He's just a tiny one. He's fully mature, very healthy, and clearly a little lover."

I swear the woman has hearts in her eyes when she looks at any of these cats. I get it for this one, certainly.

A low trilling meow comes from Colin's arms and he bends to release Goob, who trots over looking rather spry compared to how curmudgeonly and creaky he normally seems. He brushes along my pant leg—thank goodness Andy has lint rollers at the exit—and sniffs along Snickerdoodle's whiskers, then meanders to a nearby cushion and plunks down.

"They have really bonded lately. It's possible they'll have some challenges transitioning to single-cat homes, but you'll be around a lot initially, at least, right?" Andy's tapping through something on a tablet, likely the information she runs through for every adoption. "They've been pretty inseparable."

Her bright blue eyes find mine and she gives me what I can only describe as a weighty look. I raise my brows like "what?" and she simply flutters her lashes and smiles.

I don't know what this means, but I feel a little squiggly and antsy inside. I can't take Goob *and* Snickerdoodle, and I think I'd break Colin's heart if I tried. He's so matter-of-fact about the adoption it feels like he was destined for the mangey orange long-hair.

But there's an insinuation in her cheery, fake-innocent gaze.

The woman has cat-matching superpowers, runs such an ethical setup, and has saved dozens of little cat lives already in the short time she's been operating. She's amazing.

She's also kind of sneaky and I wonder if she's somehow up to something, though I can't figure out what that'd be.

Finally, I realize she did ask me a question and figure she may need to know the answer as a part of the adoption process.

"Yes. I'm taking off work for the holidays, so I'll be at home, but even when I start back, I have freedom and obviously I live nearby and often eat lunch at home." It's not the most glamorous answer and there's a little yelp of embarrassment trying to climb into my brain, but I ignore it.

Colin isn't like my parents—he doesn't care about the "optics" of things. In fact, he's typically pretty insistent on practicality and choices that make sense for real life in a way I found refreshing even as a kid. Where my parents might see my going home for lunch as a missed networking opportunity or a sign my business is failing, Colin won't. I know it.

When I glance up at him, he's studying me with a crease in his brow.

"You good?"

He blinks out of the trance he was evidently caught in and nods. "All good." He turns to Andy. "What else do you need from us?"

After a few more minutes of kitty cuddles and promises to see them again, we finish up the paperwork and work on lint-rolling and washing hands. In a matter of a half hour, we're back on the street just outside the bright pink door, and I'm all set to be a cat owner.

I'm borderline giddy as I pace down the sidewalk, then back. "I don't know how I'm supposed to go back to work now. I need to go to a pet store and get supplies. I need to cat-proof my house. I need to—" Then I launch at him.

And it's the momentum of the adrenaline and excitement and the feelings brewing over a lifelong dream being realized because he gave me the nudge under the guise of a gift, but I wrap my arms around his shoulders and kiss his cheek. Then I do it again, and I don't stop peppering his cheek and jaw with kisses, hugging him and feeling so light and excited, I should probably be worried.

It's only when he turns, almost like he wants the little pecks to end somewhere else, that I stop, my breath catching in my throat.

"So I guess you liked the present?" he asks, his voice low and his gaze deliciously intent on me. His hands are pressing into my back over the layers of clothing and the wool of my coat.

I have a flash of holding on to him without all of this between us and release him, blinking away the fantasy and begging my heart to steady. I don't want that ache sneaking in now while I'm floating. I don't want the bitter with this sweet.

"Yes. I very much do. There's a weird sense of relief, but also..." I shake my head, searching for how to describe it. "I don't know, it's like I'm embarrassed by how happy this is making me. Like, maybe I shouldn't be this excited over adopting a cat, or like the fact that I am makes it even more pathetic that I never did this for myself."

And oof, saying it out loud makes me want to shrivel up right here on the sidewalk and melt despite the chilly temps.

His expression shifts from the warm, pleased one to concern and what might be frustration. "No guilting or shaming yourself. This is about doing something you've wanted to do, and of course, feel your feelings or whatever you need to do, but don't let anything make you feel bad for the choices you've made."

I snort an indelicate laugh. "You say that like we can all live regret-free. Are you really saying you don't have regrets?"

I realize the gravity of the question the instant it's fully formed, but there's no taking it back. And sure, I feel regret over not having gotten a cat sooner, that I let myself hesitate for so long for whatever reason, but the larger issue is instantly there.

Do you regret disappearing? Which time? Do you regret leaving me behind? Do you regret living so much of this life without me?

I expect him to laugh it off, but I shouldn't. I know Colin and thankfully, the version of him standing with me doesn't run.

Instead, he steps close and waits until I meet his gaze. His stern expression tells me there's no quip on the horizon.

"I have a lot of regrets, CP. I can't even begin to pretend I don't. Being here with you these last few weeks has drilled that home more than anything else."

My mouth is dry. I try to swallow. I don't have words.

He keeps going. "But I think sometimes, we can do something about those regrets."

His gorgeous eyes have mine locked into his and I can't look away. My heart is fluttering and I want to scream "so, what are you going to do about yours?" But somehow, I manage to say, "Like finally getting a cat."

A smile tugs at his lips. "Yeah, CP. Like finally getting a cat."

CHAPTER TWENTY-ONE

Colin

Janie opens the door and rifles through a tiny bag she's holding without looking up.

It's a mercy she's looking down because I can't breathe. She's always beautiful and I knew she'd look incredible tonight, but damn.

She's wearing something gold, or maybe she'd call it champagne. It's light enough it almost looks like the color of her perfect, creamy skin. It cuts into a halter, tying behind her neck, and fits her lithe body in a sheath all the way to the floor. I see bright red pumps at the bottom, bright red nails on her fingers, and then stunningly simple makeup. Her bright eyes are smoky and darker than normal when she lifts her head.

Her hair is pulled back at the sides, then hangs in a wavy dark curtain at her back.

I cough. "You're—you're beautiful. Stunning."

She beams. "Thank you. You look very handsome. This is..." She takes in the numerous medals and ropes and badges and pins adorning my mess dress uniform. "I'm always amazed at how much you guys have to wear on the jacket part."

She leans in and touches the tip of one finger to one of the shining brass buttons affixing the jacket at my waist. I don't love this uniform because it is so stiff and formal, but I don't mind her eyes on me in it.

Maybe it's not all bad.

"Help me with my coat?"

She turns and slips a hand through the fabric she's holding up. I rush to help settle it around her shoulders. The long black wool coat has a belt she's now tying, cinching in at her slim waist, and is surprisingly soft.

I help her into the car, though she doesn't need it. Too bad, because I'm looking for any excuse to touch her. I'd already planned to dance at least once, but now I'm thinking I might be interested in more than one song, if she's up for it.

We make small talk in the car and I've never been happier we're taking a rideshare than when she reaches for my hand and holds it, lacing our fingers together while she gazes at me and I tell her a little more what to expect.

We enter the hotel ballroom and the space is packed. It's a far larger group here than the last gathering since this is a huge brigade-level function, which means hundreds of soldiers invited, plus partners, rather than just a few dozen.

"Everyone looks amazing," Janie says in a breathy way that snags my attention.

When I glance over at her, her eyes are brimming.

"Uh, you okay?" I guide her to the far right, dodging the receiving line to see what's going on.

She chuckles and dabs a finger at the corner of each eye, gently sniffing away the emotion. "I'm sorry. It's so sentimental and cheesy, but sometimes I think about all the things this community has done and it's just incredible. I don't know what it's like to be a military family member or spouse, but it's just..." She shakes her head, her eyes darting around before they settle on mine. "It's an honor to be here with you. And I know you're going to cringe, but thank you."

"Thank you?"

She bites her lip, a glint of mischief entering her gaze, and she stage-whispers, "For your service."

I cringe dramatically just for her. She rewards me with a boisterous laugh that's better than a glass of champagne.

I take her hand in mine, more than a little pleased we've gotten so comfortable with this level of physical contact, and guide us toward the coat check. I help her out of the soft garment and try not to swallow my tongue when I see the back of her stunning gown. The back cuts low—not inappropriate, but more of her back than I've seen since we were teens in swimsuits. I had trouble keeping my eyes on my own paper then, too, but now, I'm wondering how I'm supposed to make it through this in one piece.

Just then, I see Josh walk by and send me flashing brows followed by an obnoxious wink, almost like he's saying, *You're not. That's what I was trying to tell you, man.*

He veers toward us, but Janie's looking the other direction. He pats my shoulder and whispers, "She brings out the best in you."

Surprisingly heartfelt considering the gleam in his eye, but I'm relieved Janie was busy waving to someone she met at the last event and didn't see it.

The cat present went as well as I hoped, and I've

resolved to accept my fate. I'm not sure I can do anything else. I've loved this woman for nearly my entire life and spending time with her now has changed nothing. If anything, it's made my desire to know her more deeply, to be tethered to her indefinitely and in a final, lasting way, more intense.

So tonight, I'll savor every minute of this. The fact that it makes our marriage look real is a bonus at this point, not the mission.

"What now?" she asks, turning to find me staring longingly at her back like a creep.

"Receiving line."

We move through the line, greeting each command team and their spouses, shaking hands in the oldest, worst military ball custom in my humble opinion. Janie, to no one's surprise, is absolutely charming and makes me look far more personable than I would've on my own.

Then, we're free to scuttle past the towering fake Christmas trees with white lights and golden balls and snowflake décor and head straight for the cash bar where I grab her a cocktail and introduce her to a few people I know. Josh wanders over and we chat. I silently transmit the order for him not to embarrass me, but since he is actually my best friend and not just someone who enjoys torturing me, he doesn't.

The emcee calls us to dinner and the formal portion begins. We stand for the presenting of colors, the introduction and thanks to the special guests, the procedural toasts to include spotlighting the fallen comrade table for those lost.

There's always a moment at these things when I remember years past when they'd flash up photos and read names, when the ones lost were lists of soldiers who'd died on the most recent deployment. It sent all of this into a harsh glare, the hubris of celebrating and drinking and dancing when so many others didn't make it home to do so. But it's been years since those days, and tonight, the most persistent ache in my heart is eased.

Because the person I've always longed for, the person I've always *missed,* sometimes when she was right beside me because I knew it wouldn't last, is here with me.

The speaker is mercifully brief and soon, we're all chatting over dinner, then slowly finishing desserts and taking places on the dance floor.

The time has come, and I'm more than ready to be close to Janie without a table full of people studying us.

She sets her hand on my shoulder and the other in mine. When I settle my palm against her bare shoulder blade, every cell in my body wakes up, especially when her breath catches.

Then we move.

It's not the first time we've danced together. She'd wanted me to take her to my prom, and then to hers, but in every case, her parents refused to allow it. I'd always known I wasn't good enough for her in their eyes, but it was high school before it sank in completely.

She refused to accept the invitation from a son of her parents' friends and instead went with a group of girls. I'd been relieved, but still jealous anyone might get to dance with her.

But she came and found me, then demanded I dance just one song with her. Of course I didn't refuse. I'd never had a good excuse to be that close to her and I couldn't imagine a time when I would again. She was wearing this soft pink ballgown with a poofy skirt and her hair was pulled up into a fancy style on her head complete with tiara.

I remember thinking how perfectly it fit. She really had looked like a princess.

And then there was the night we got married. That was a different, more casual setting. Boy band music and too much champagne. Less formal.

"The last time I danced at a military ball, it was with my cousin," she says, a smile gracing her perfect lips.

"Oh, I bet that was a party." I don't know Will Gruff all that well, but he always seemed like one of those guys who took things super seriously. His demeanor at Andy's Place was unexpectedly cheery, though after interacting with the woman herself a few times, I imagine it would be hard to maintain anything but lightness around her.

In fact, this is the way I function around Janie. Josh has even mentioned it.

Over the years, I've been severe at times. On myself, on my soldiers, and on my peers. Josh has seen me at my worst in that regard, and his whispered comment tonight that Janie brings out the best in me? It hit home.

Because he's right.

I feel it in my gut. The way I'm more concerned with the feel of her warm, smooth skin under my palm than how I look in the eyes of my commanding officers I haven't developed a rapport with is one clear sign. But the other is that I'm not nervous about the ball. The twisting, leaping sensation in my gut is all about *her* and where this might go instead of a dull anxiety building to a roar as the night goes on about how my career will or won't pan out.

"What are you thinking about?"

She leans in and I'm happy to gather her close as I say,

"I was thinking about the last time we danced like this." I don't stop, don't keep my distance like I probably should.

Instead, I let my lips graze the shell of her ear when I add, "I used to dream we'd dance again. Still did, even after Vegas."

The breath whooshes out of her and she shakes her head, but instead of easing out of my arms, which I dread, she presses closer and holds me tighter, too.

She arches a brow, humor flickering in her expression. "Dream come true, then?"

I nod, meaning every word. "Dream come true, CP."

CHAPTER TWENTY-TWO

Janie

We've been dancing for almost an hour.

My feet hurt. My face hurts from smiling and laughing with him.

In truth? My heart hurts a little.

I'm trying with all my might to resist. I really am. But dang if the man isn't wooing me when he doesn't even mean to. He's saying all these sweet things and connecting our past with our present. I should love it.

I *do* love it.

But it also just... hurts.

He was thinking about the first time we danced and now I am. I'm remembering how pretty I felt and how I begged my parents to let me take him as my date. They didn't just suggest it would be awkward since he didn't go to my school or how renting a tux might be a financial stretch—nothing so subtle.

I'll never forget my mother turning beet red and my father slowly lowering his newspaper and sliding down his reading glasses to say, "Let's be honest, Janie. It's beneath you."

It's beneath you. At the very least, they didn't say *he* was beneath me, but of course that's what they meant. I realized this more fully when my mother added, "When you marry, you'll do it with someone like you. And we might as well be practicing that now, right?"

We. Also, why were they talking about marriage?

So I'd asked him if he'd meet me after. If maybe we could sneak into his back yard and steal a moment for ourselves. When he met me at their wooden gate door, his eyes skated over me in the most thrilling, obvious way. He had to clear his throat twice before he spoke. He'd put on black pants and a blue button-down and a tie.

Dancing with him tonight feels oddly similar to our dance over a decade ago. My heart was breaking a little that night because I loved him and I wanted him in more ways than we'd admitted, and he would be leaving for the military academy soon. The reality that this was all I'd get from him felt so clear then, even as my little heart had churned out hope after hope.

But haven't I been hoping like that for years?

Haven't I fooled myself into having something to hope for beyond just the moment time and again? Throughout our teen years, all of his college years at the academy wondering if *this* would be the Christmas he'd be home for long enough to visit me, for months after he commissioned and started active duty. Then years of rejecting the hope only to have it cruelly rekindled in Vegas.

At least I didn't hang on so long that time. He disappeared on me, drew the line thick as a wall, and I didn't even try to cross it afterward.

But now?

I'm so twisted up in hopes, I'm a braid. I've twined myself around the dual threads of love and hope and I've tried to resist, but here we are. I'm in his arms and he's smiling at me, looking at me like I'm everything he's ever wanted and I'm both the happiest I've been in so long and teetering on an edge I'm scared may destroy me.

"I think I need to give my feet a break," I say, easing back from him as another slow song starts. My feet are toast, yes, but I can't endure circling the dance floor to "I'll Be Home For Christmas" with this man. Not right now. I just can't.

"Me, too. Shockingly, patent leather dress shoes are not the most comfortable." He rests a hand to usher me toward our table, his thumb brushing the exposed skin just above where the material of the dress cuts across my lower back.

After we sit for a minute, Josh saunters over and crouches down between us, hands balancing himself in place on the chair backs.

"Time to go get your photo. Santa's only here for another twenty minutes, but the line's moving quickly."

This doesn't compute for me, but Colin's already shaking his head.

"No, I don't think so."

"Um, no to you, sir. Absolutely yes."

Colin glares at Josh.

Josh mean-mugs Colin right back.

"Can someone explain? Why are we saying no to Santa?"

Josh snaps and points at me, which seems to be his

signature move. "Exactly. *Who* says no to Santa this time of year? I mean, are you willing to risk getting put on the naughty list?"

I chuckle. Colin looses an aggrieved sigh.

"Fine. We'll go. You've bullied us into it." Then he stands and holds his hand out for me. "But now, we're fully committing. Whatever cheesy prom-style pose they ask of us, we're doing it, and we're going to be damn sincere about it, too."

I don't fully grasp his meaning until we queue up in a short line and I get a glimpse at the setup. There are two different scenes set up with green screen backgrounds and a few live props in front—the first features, as Josh promised, Santa himself in a rocking chair and a high-backed leather chair next to him. All around the bottom are shiny wrapped packages in various shades of red, green, white, and gold.

The next scene a few feet away features a large Christmas tree and nothing else from what I can see.

"Maybe this'll make up for never getting real prom photos. You think?" He lifts his chin toward the ho-ho-hoeing Santa as he greets the next guests right in front of us.

"Oh, definitely."

"Ho! Ho! Ho! Who do we have here? Come on over with Santa and get a photo for your scrapbook," Santa says, waving us over with a be-gloved hand.

With one last shared look of amusement, Colin and I follow the jolly man's orders.

"Now, sir, you sit down, and we'll have the missus perch on your knee."

Then it's all happening fast, and publicly. Colin's seated and I'm settling in on his lap. He's instructed to settle one hand around my waist which feels oddly intimate right now, and then he's lacing our fingers together with his other. It's a very odd pose.

"Now Santa's going to stand next to you here. Don't mind me as I get into place," Santa narrates as he sets up just behind us, from what I can tell.

Someone counts down and they snap a few photos. I wish I'd handed off my phone to a person waiting in line because I'm not sure when we'll get to see this composition, and I have a feeling it'll lighten my mood even further.

"Now we'll have one of you two sit on Santa's knee!"

This sounds suspiciously like Josh's voice, and then he's there, ushering Santa back into his chair, taking my hand and urging me into the leather seat on my own, and giggling —yes, the grown man in his dashing military uniform is full-on giggling—as he settles Colin onto Santa's lap.

It's Santa's "Oh!" that breaks my composure.

A little snort ekes out because Colin's face is sugar plum purple and he's glaring at Josh, who's scuttling out of the way and saying, "Take it! Take that picture!"

I cover my mouth to avoid cackling at the sight of my gorgeous date perched on Santa's knee, clearly stunned by Josh's manufactured whirlwind.

"Got it! You folks can head on to the next scene. Enjoy!" The photographer of the Santa scene waves us over to the now-empty setup.

I pop up but not before Colin does, eyes rolling and searching for Josh, who has conveniently disappeared.

We don't even have a second to give each other a "wow, that was a lot" shared look before the person assisting the next photographer is positioning Colin, straightening his shoulders and then nudging me into his side, just in front of him.

"Wrap your hands around her waist now. Good. Yes. Right over top. Beautiful."

We're posed in what has to be one of the worst ways—he's behind me, arms around me, hands on top of mine, which are at essentially my belly. I'm not particularly self-conscious about my body and even I am second-guessing whether I look pregnant and this is supposed to celebrate my non-existent baby bump.

I'm still laughing at the image of Colin on Santa's lap, and I hope with everything in me the photo comes out. I'll hang it on my fridge. In an alternate universe where we're actually married for good, I'd send it out as a Christmas card to everyone we've ever met.

We stand in the pose while the camera clicks, undoubtedly smiling awkwardly, and then she repositions us so we're facing and holding hands. Also pretty terrible, because we're facing each other and perpendicular to the camera, but our faces are turned toward the lens. It's borderline painful, and again, deeply awkward.

"I suspect these will be the best pictures I've ever taken," Colin says from behind his smile.

I giggle, but keep smiling, straining. "The ones with Santa will never be topped, but for the two of us, yes. Absolutely. Me, too."

"Okay, perfect, and now, kiss!"

We've relaxed a touch but are still holding hands when I see the assistant walk out with a long pole, a string tied to the end, and at the bottom, the poisonous little weed that is mistletoe is fastened to the tip. It bobs between us, right above our foreheads.

Colin must be in denial because he asks, "Kiss?"

"Mistletoe!" the assistant says, beaming and waving the

plant around like a prized fish before she swings it back toward us.

"Do it! Do it! Do it!"

Past the beaming spotlights on us, I think I can see Josh pumping his arm.

Nerves sizzle and burst in my chest as my eyes find Colin's. But there's no terror there. He's shaking his head and saying, "Sorry. I'll make this up to you somehow right after I murder him," then leaning in.

I do, too, because I haven't completely forgotten why we're here. What if his commander is watching? What if someone thinks we don't look like a real husband and wife? What if I ruin everything by backing away and saying I don't want to kiss him in front of all of these people because we have to?

So I lean in and press my lips to his. I wait, counting, hardly able to enjoy the contact, and force a laugh when we hear, "Great job. Super cute, you two," from the architect of this nightmare.

Then I bolt. Not run, but I use every bit of the advantage my five-ten height gives me and I move toward the restrooms, tossing something about taking a moment before I start crying.

Because the tears are coming, and I'm trying not to lose it entirely. I'm mentally packing it away, shoving down the longing and disappointment threatening to topple me. The swing from hilarity to *this* is too much.

I should've let myself live in the fantasy of tonight, but Colin gave me the exact reminder I needed to stay tethered to reality.

He reminded me of prom. Reminded me of that longing and heartbreak, of how he *always* ends up leaving, and how I cannot lose myself to that process again.

By the time I emerge from the bathroom a few minutes later, I've refreshed my lipstick and banished the handful of tears that snuck out against my permission. I've pulled my shoulders back, tightened my core, and reminded myself I'm a badass woman who can handle this.

I can, I will, and I must.

So I get back out there, paste on a smile, and I do.

CHAPTER TWENTY-THREE

Colin

Janie's been off for the last hour or so, but I'm not sure what to do to get us back on track.

We had fun, didn't we? The photos were a bit much, but she seemed to get a kick out of seeing me on Santa's lap and I'd do anything if it makes her laugh like that. Obviously, the mistletoe kiss was all wrong, but it's kind of hilarious. And it only makes me look forward to kissing her *without* an audience.

Every touch. Every glance. It's all made me feel closer to her and like I can't get close enough. After so long just *wishing*, I've moved to thinking maybe this can actually happen.

Maybe we could have a moment together without an audience. Enjoy this closeness we've committed to.

I had been hoping that might work out tonight, when I

dropped her off. Maybe she'd invite me in and we'd spend time together.

But now that we're in the rideshare on the way to her house, I feel far less clear about whether that's even a possibility.

I've never had this kind of fun at a military ball, and I want her to know it's because of her. Everything good about tonight is all her.

Anytime I go to speak, though, she's looking out the window like she's never seen the city. Her neck's strained away and though we're holding hands, she's barely present in the car with me.

We're holding hands and it feels like that means something. There's no one to see. No one policing our behavior. But she's put up walls with her silence and her body language. It leaves me feeling like I've lost the path forward and I'm turning around, wondering where I am.

Where are we?

I know where I want to be. I know it more clearly than I ever have, and for the first time, it feels possible. We're married, and not for a night. We're together, and yes, it's part of an agreement, but it's more. Our fingers threaded together prove that. I'm not even about to leave due to my work—I'm *here*. And it's the first time since I graduated high school I can honestly say I'll be in her space and my career ambitions aren't getting in the way of a future.

It's possible.

But she's locked up tight. I don't know how to get in and explore what she wants, which is ultimately all that matters.

What I would've done in the past is pulling at me—*just leave. She doesn't want you. She hates all of this faking. You're not good enough.*

But I hear Josh and even Lina in my head. I know the reality staring me in the face.

I can leave now and effectively end things between us. It'll show I plan to do what I've always done—protect myself—when this is all truly over. The obligations on my side of the deal are done and she could cancel hers, or we can move through the motions at her family event to check the box and then part ways and never look back.

But how has that worked for me? It hasn't. Yes, I've protected myself, but have I gained anything? Have I managed any other real relationships that had a future? Have I managed to leave the longing for her in the past and see a way forward with anyone else?

No. I haven't. And in my gut, I've always known it's because I've wanted it to be her. More than that, on a soul-deep level, I think I know it's always going to be her for me.

The question is, am I it for her?

I don't know that, but I will never know if I can't stand my ground and hash it out. If I keep running under the guise of protecting myself or protecting her, I've lost.

So when the driver pulls up to her curb, I get out. I make no show of asking him to take me to my place, instead following her to the door, and as she turns, holding her breath, I tuck a strand of hair that's fallen from her style behind her ear.

"Can I come in?"

Her eyes bounce to mine. "Um, I—"

"Not like, *come in* come in, just to talk."

She bites her lip, a furrow at her brows, but nods. "Okay."

Not exactly the winning endorsement one might hope for, but I'll take it. We would get to the bottom of things tonight.

She lets us in and hangs her coat in the hallway closet. I realize I can finally remove my jacket and happily do so, hanging it, too. I'm still deeply uncomfortable, but I slip my shoes off and bask in that freedom, promising myself I'll wear nothing but cotton tomorrow to make up for all the polyester of this uniform.

"Would you like some water?" She flips on lights in the living room and kitchen, then moves to cabinets after setting her purse on the corner of the white marble counter.

"Sure. That'd be great." I look around, admiring her space as she fills the glasses.

Her kitchen is all clean lines but manages to feel cozy. I'm not even sure how—maybe it's the butcher block island in the middle, or some of the accents she has. It doesn't surprise me it feels more stylish and yet lived-in than almost any other house I've been to.

The living room is equally stylish and warm. It's clean and classic, with homey colors like sage and forest greens, woods and creams and other touches I don't have the language for but still put me at ease. It invites me in to look and admire, but it also says, "You're welcome here."

"Your home is beautiful, Janie."

She hands me a glass. "Thank you."

"Let's sit. I'm sure we're both ready to be off our feet for at least a day." It's a sorry attempt at a joke, but I'm not sure how to do this. I've never made myself stay and talk through the discomfort, and now that I'm here, I don't know exactly where to start.

Janie is uncharacteristically silent. We're in her house and she should be pointing out different pieces of art and the memories attached—because knowing her, there's a good reason for each part of this living room and it's not purely based on aesthetics.

I take a deep breath, hoping to do this right. "So. Something happened." Not a fantastic first effort, but it's a beginning.

Her brows tent and she looks at me, but she still doesn't speak. She's going to make me do all the work here, and I can't blame her for it.

"I don't know what changed tonight. It seemed like we were having a great time, and then something shifted. I'm not sure what. I want to figure it out and fix it."

Her frown deepens and she studies her fingers for a few moments. The bright red polish is still shiny and perfect, and her hands are, like the rest of her, beautiful.

"I know I've done something wrong, CP. Help me understand what it was."

She shakes her head and a small sigh escapes. "I can't do this with you."

"Can't do what?"

She straightens, more energy coming off her now than there has been for the last hour. "*This.* I can't have these moments of closeness and connection and then watch you walk away *again*."

A chain with links made of regret, frustration, and resignation wraps around me and I accept her words as best I can. It's a vise squeezing, slowly, inevitably.

"There we go. I knew this would catch up with me, and I can't blame you for feeling that way."

I run a hand through my hair, wondering how much of the truth I should share now. It's too much to hit her with the full reality of my decisions, the truest motivation, but I can share with her something that might give her an inkling into my mindset.

"I told you I regret walking away as a kid—and let's make sure we're acknowledging I truly was a child. I entered the academy at eighteen and I was terrified and lonely and angry and lost." It's about as cliché as it comes, but anger drove me more than anything else.

My dad went to jail—anger.

I couldn't be with the girl I wanted—anger.

I didn't know how to manage my life or how to compensate for what I saw as all the faults of my family and upbringing and *self*—so much anger.

"I nearly lost my spot at the school the first semester because I was so homesick." Or heartsick. For her. "But Josh and one of our mentors set me straight and I realized I couldn't plan to go home and be reminded of him." *And of you,* my helpful brain adds. "I convinced myself I wouldn't succeed if I kept looking back. So I went hard the other way, and I did the least possible to stay tethered to my past and who I was. That meant cutting so many ties and failing you and my family. I will never stop being sorry I couldn't figure out how to balance things."

She dips her head in a small nod. "I don't blame you. I did then, on and off, but that's not the part that makes me feel like this is all heading toward me being left again." Her voice shakes and she presses her fingers to her lips for a moment as though to steady them. "We made a choice in Vegas and it might've been fueled by too much tequila and champagne, but..." She sighs and her shoulders slump like she's lost all her steam.

I slip a hand around her neck and let my thumb stroke along her smooth skin. "Tell me."

"I don't think I can do it again. And all of this pretending... I thought maybe I'd be able to keep it all separate. We'd be friends and play like it's more, but turns out I'm not that strong."

My pulse ticks up at this admission and I want to smash my lips to hers, but I don't. Because I have more to do here.

"I've never only wanted to be your friend, CP. I've always wanted more and that's always been at play for me. What I want to say now—what I'd like you to consider—is whether you can trust me enough to give this a real shot."

She blinks, but I've hurt her too much too many times, so I keep going.

"Think about whether you might want to really try together. And if any part of you does, you say the word, and I'm in. I know I've got to show you that—I've got to prove to you that I won't disappear on you again. I'm more than ready to do that, if you want me to. But if all of this between us, our history, has added up to me letting you down too many times, I get that, too. I will not blame you. But I need you to decide and let me know."

Her lashes flutter and her mouth opens, then shuts. She's not just surprised by these words, she's stunned.

Inevitably, it charms me, and I pull her in to press a kiss into her temple.

"I'll see you tomorrow to get the cats, right?" I stand, determined to give her space and not take any more from her that she doesn't want to give.

Once I've slipped on my shoes and I'm pulling on my jacket, she's hustling to the door.

"Thank you. I'll think about it. I promise."

I nod, accepting that. It's all I can ask, and it's more than generous for her to give.

CHAPTER TWENTY-FOUR

Janie

The term "sleepless night" is a cutesy little thing someone termed when they tossed and turned a bit.

Last night, I experienced what I'm not-so-fondly thinking of as a sleepless eternity condensed into one endless six-hour period. By five this morning, I surrendered. After a jog—terrible by the way, because see the whole "not sleeping" situation—and force-feeding myself some yogurt and coffee, I feel like burnt toast.

The only thing keeping me moving is the promise of bringing my cat home today. I'm a bit fluttery thinking of it, actually, and it's definitely the cat who has me in a tizzy and not the prospect of seeing Colin again.

Definitely not Colin.

I mean, *obviously* not him.

Because I cannot stomach the thought of being antsy

and excited to see him after reliving the entire *decade* of time that passed in the window between when he left my house last night and this morning when I rolled out of bed feeling beaten up and haggard.

My brain traveled every possible little anxious pathway it could.

What would it look like to be with him the way he seems to want?

Then I'd have a little party-slash-freak-out and replay our conversation. Me saying I don't think I can do it again and unfortunately revisiting the dread and absolute ache filling up my body like cement in a fish tank. Then his, *"I've always wanted more,"* tossed out so... so... casually. Like they weren't words I'd longed for and begged for internally. Like I hadn't dreamed of them.

Why now? I mean, yes, we're married. So that's one aspect. But why not any moment before now? Why not?

"Ughgh!" I nearly scream it, but that would take more energy than I have right now as I slip outside and shiver in the cold December air. My breath gusts out in white puffs and my face is instantly chilly.

The temperature helps me focus. I have a ten-minute walk. Colin's bringing his car since he lives farther away. The plan is for us to ride together back to my house and he'll drop off me and Snickerdoodle and then he'll continue on with Goob.

There's a little twinge of regret that we'll be separating the two cats. There'll be some major adjusting. Andy even mentioned they don't always let cats go alone as younger adults, but since Goob is older, and they know me, she's allowing it.

I wish they could stay together. I've had the thought

more than once, but I won't voice it. I can't. Because what that means is something bigger than cats.

And it has me circling right back around to what I'm supposed to be considering. Surely, he knows I won't have decided whether I can wrap my head around being with him for real in the matter of a night. Right?

I wish I could've. But every time I thought of his sweet words, the sincerity coating every syllable, I also vividly remembered all the times he'd left. And he acknowledged that, thank goodness. But am I the kind of woman who's that brave? Or is it something I want to be brave about, but would actually be horribly and unforgivably stupid of me?

When I see him standing outside Andy's Place, cheeks flushed from the cold and eyes pinned on my approach, my heart rate picks up.

There's no denying I'm attracted to him or that my feelings are growing. They were already kind of a mess, but they're expanding out so rapidly, I can't help but feel cautious.

"Morning," he says, raising an arm for a hug and drawing me into his warmth.

He's wearing jeans and a sweater with a sporty black winter jacket unzipped. When I indulge in the embrace, a coffee, pine, and peppermint scent mixed with clean soap and laundry and warm skin downright intoxicates me. It sends my pulse thrumming in my veins, but it somehow relaxes me, too.

Rather emblematic of the man himself.

It wouldn't be at all weird for me to stand here with my arms around him and inhale this scent for another ten minutes or so, would it? *Asking for a friend.*

"Morning," I manage, finally tearing myself away from his heat and heavenly scent.

The hug is... good. And the proximity to him feels *so* good. He always looks so appealing, and he's got this expression that says he'll be patient with me.

I want so badly to believe it.

But he'll cut and run. It's an echo inside me, not even a thought. It's the reality of memory taking root and trying to conjure up the proof of lessons already learned.

He holds the door, so I slip in, relieved to be greeted by the tangy pine fragrance wafting from the squatty Christmas tree just inside and the peppermint coffee smell. *Huh.* Maybe he'd been here a while before I arrived?

"Yay! You're here! Are we ready?" Andy claps her hands together, delight emanating from her, and she waves at us as she calls, "Meet you up there!"

Then it's all happening in rapid succession. Andy gets the cats loaded up into the carriers, which Colin apparently brought in earlier. We finalize the paperwork, signing just before we take the cats to the car. Then we're driving, and my pulse is erratic.

How am I so happy, but I feel so torn up about this? Why do I feel like he's leaving again?

I remind myself I had negative one thousand hours of sleep last night and my logic tools are failing me. I'm emotional because it's a big day, a dream is coming true, and yet we're also separating these kitties. Goob sits squatty and silent in his cage as though he knows what's happening, but my guy is yowling with an edge of despair mixed with suspicion, a sound that says he's pretty sure we're taking him to add his pretty mottled fur to a coat a Disney villain will wear.

"You're alright, buddy. We're almost there." The drive is short but clearly longer than either cat particularly wanted to endure, and it's all so fast, I haven't even sorted out what to say to Colin by the time we pull up in front of my place.

"Need help in?" he asks, jogging around the car to open the back door and pull out Snickerdoodle's cage since I've already exited the passenger side.

"No, we'll be fine. Get Goob home and settled." I lean in and press a kiss to his cheek as he hands me the cage.

Snickerdoodle looses a stressed meow.

"You better get him inside." He leans down, placing his face just outside. "You're in good hands, my friend. You're a lucky guy."

For some reason, this cracks me open just a little. The combination of exhaustion and fear and longing and a touch of stress knowing my new cat is losing his mind in this cage makes me certain I'm in danger of bawling right here on the sidewalk if I don't get inside and away from this man.

He shuts the door as I move away with every intention of making space between us so I can breathe.

"Let me know how he's doing later," he calls.

I pause at the door, unlocking it with a sense of surrealism I haven't experienced before. Everything slows down but my heart speeds up.

He's so thoughtful. He's tenderhearted just like he always was, and he says he wants this. But I can't live like this. I can't handle the way I feel like any time I turn around, he might have disappeared.

It's unwise to say anything when I can feel my body and brain at war with themselves and fueled by a deranged sense of sleep-deprived anxiety, but I can't stop myself once I've turned and set my eyes on him.

"I think maybe we should take some time. Until the party at my parents' house. Let's just get some space."

And from there, I don't even let myself take in his expression as I fumble through the door and walk straight to the laundry room where I'm going to let Snickerdoodle set up shop. I set him down and take gulping breaths in and promise myself this is the best thing for all of us.

M.O.M. NETWORK

Mothers Of Military Network Message board:

CoolyKay: Updates? News?

Vic: Progress stalled out. They went to the military ball, lovely time, and then she asked for space. I think it's starting to seem real. He said he laid it out there, though I know he didn't tell her everything. But she asked for space until her family's party.

SCLDG: These children. Exhaustingly obtuse.

JusticeLVR: Oh, come on. They're humans. Love is scary, especially if it's a long time coming.

CoolyKay: Well, isn't that the truth?

Vic: I'm worried if they don't see each other until this party, that's going to ruin it. He's never felt comfortable with her family and they're not exactly welcoming. They need more time!

CoolyKay: What can we do?

JusticeLVR: Let's get unhinged with this—how about a strategic little tiny fire in his apartment so he has to move in with her? Forced proximity, anyone? I put mine in the same room for Christmas and scandalized them—worked like a charm.

Vic: Maybe let's not do something that could get us sent to jail? My family has a bit of a rough history with that.

JusticeLVR: Right. Sorry.

SCLDG: I have an idea.

Vic: …

CoolyKay: Love it. Yes.

SCLDG: I haven't even said what it is.

JusticeLVR: We trust you.

Vic: I'd like a hint, at least. I'm not the blindly trusting type, as much as I love you all.

SCLDG: I know someone who knows someone who can get information to someone who might be able to create a scenario where they have to spend a little time together ASAP.

JusticeLVR: Mysterious.

CoolyKay: Thrilling!

Vic: … What are the odds of jail time?

CHAPTER TWENTY-FIVE

Colin

Goob and I find a routine so quickly, it's hard to remember he hasn't grown old with me.

Our unit's working half days now that we're in the final days before the holiday, so I've only left him for a few hours at a time.

Whenever I return to the house, he hops down from wherever he's perched and trots over to me, brushes against my leg and instantly starts purring, and I pick him up for some cuddles.

The only snag we've hit is that the guy doesn't like to be brushed. The one and only time he's swatted at or bit me was when I tried to brush the somewhat matted fur on his back toward his tail end. *Not a fan.* I don't want him getting furballs so I'm still working on him, trying different brushes and approaches, and generally letting this elderly man of a cat distract me from the fact that I haven't talked to or heard from Janie in any way since Sunday.

It's now Thursday.

It's been stupidly painful to have this radio silence between us. I should be embarrassed by the thought, but I keep thinking it was easier when I imposed the distance between us. Then I berate myself because of course it was, and thinking about that makes me a jackass. My idiot choice to run from her and stay gone in every sense so many times is exactly why I'm in this situation.

I don't blame her for needing space. What I'm not sure about is what to do about it.

I can't show her I'm not going anywhere if I'm not near her. I can't show her I'm being faithful to my promise to engage and be invested if we're miles apart.

In the long run, I'm in DC and I can be *right here* for her.

I've been running through different options in my head all week. I'll see her again on December twenty-fifth. That's the day of the family party at her parents' house. It border-line kills me I won't get to see her on Christmas Eve, but if I'm respecting her desire for space, then I won't see her until the twenty-fifth.

"I have to respect her wishes, right? This isn't a time where I can show her I'm all in by ignoring them and showing up at her place, is it?"

Goob, who's currently curled into a ball on my belly, blinks open one eye, closes it again, and snuzzles his little face back into his paws.

"Fine. Message received. I'll listen to her words and not try to read her mind or assume I know what's best." I glare at him for a solid minute before I cave and pet his back, which lights the fire of his purr and he rumbles happily.

My eyes fall closed while I take this moment to be happy. It's an odd thought, but so much of my life has been about striving after something better—a better place in life, a better reputation, a better rank, better job, better assignment, better sense of self.

Right now, this little aged feline is teaching me to shut up and be.

I might like it.

An hour later, the doorbell rings and startles me awake. Goob, offended by the auditory infraction on our space, jumps down instantly, and I jog to the door. It's no surprise my heart is pounding out of my chest from the surprise, but also because there's a wild hope it might be Janie.

"Oh. It's you." I leave the door open and plod back into the apartment, leaving Josh standing at my threshold. If I had Snickerdoodle here, I'd have to watch the space for cats charging the door, but Goob is likely having a bite to eat and isn't the charge-the-door type, anyway.

"Wow. Your hospitality skills have really taken a nose-dive now that we're stateside."

He follows me. Probably.

I don't care.

"What are you doing here?"

His low chuckle is no surprise, but my bad mood kind of is. I must've dozed off with all of those happy thoughts, but I woke up with no such thing.

"I came to check on you. See what your holiday plans are." He glances around, then crouches low when Goob approaches him. "And this must be the new roommate."

I smile then, because how can I not? I mentioned I adopted a cat in passing earlier in the week and Josh instantly said he wanted to meet Goob. He's just that kind of guy—he shows up for people. He's extroverted and never afraid to be the guy who supports other people in what they're doing, even if that thing, whatever it might be, doesn't particularly interest him. It's the people that draw him.

My sisters have demanded they meet their new kitty-nephew, but I told them I wanted to let him adjust a bit more. Having been a resident of Andy's Place, he's used to attention, but I want him to feel peaceful. I know Josh won't be too demanding, whereas Bianca's kids won't contain themselves.

"That's him. A well-behaved crotchety old man," I say with a fond smile as I watch Goob rub his head along Josh's pant leg.

"Much like his owner, then." It's not a question. Purely statement.

"I'm not crotchety or old." Though in fairness, I don't have a great defense for my attitude tonight.

He clicks his tongue. "Okay. Whatever you say." He gives Goob's bright orange and cream stripes one last pat between the ears, then moves to the kitchen to wash his hands. "So tell me. What's the deal with Janie?"

I want to resist. I should tell him it's none of his business and we're still figuring things out. But I need to talk this through, and he knows me. He knows my history with Janie, and he was here less than a week ago spouting off about how I had to go for it with her because she's my one true love.

He helps himself to a water, then comes to sit. I wait until he's settled into the couch next to me before I attempt to explain what's going on.

"I laid it out after the ball. Told her I thought we should try to make this thing work for real. I explained I under-stood I'd failed her over and over again and the only way to make up for that would be to show up and stay put and just be here for her. Every time. All the time. And that I wanted her to want that, too, but she needed to think about it."

Josh is nodding, approving of my lay-it-bare approach.

"Seems wise. Vulnerable. Women love that crap."

I roll my eyes and laugh because we both know this isn't how either of us think about this kind of thing. Neither of us is a player, nor are we the kind of men who view emotional intelligence or vulnerability as a bad thing.

That said, we've both got a healthy dose of our own issues, and sometimes, that makes those things a challenge.

"Yeah. Well. After we dropped the cats off, she said she wanted space. So the next time I get to talk to her is the twenty-fifth." It hurts just saying it. I hate that it does.

"Ouch. But also, I respect her desire to think about it without having to look at you."

A laugh bursts out of me. "Ouch, thanks."

He shakes his head. "No, you're welcome. Because you're too pretty for your own good. I can understand why being near you would make it hard for her to figure out what she wants."

"Aw, you think I'm pretty?"

His turn to roll his eyes. "Sure do. But also, you should answer that." He notches his chin toward the cushion between us.

The cushion where my phone sits, the screen lit up with *Janie*.

It takes a second to register she's calling me before I scramble for the phone and accept while Josh smothers his laugh behind a meaty hand.

"Janie? Hey. Is everything okay? Are you okay?" I'm breathless and there's no way she can't hear it.

"Yes, I'm fine. But I had something come up."

My heart is hammering, mind racing, but I pull in a

breath to calm myself and get a freaking grip. "What can I do?"

She huffs a little, and the sound does stupid things to me. Then she explains. "Well, I know we're taking some time, but..."

She trails off like she expects me to object to whatever she's going to say in favor of maintaining the distance she—and definitely only she—wanted.

"I don't care about that. What do you need?"

In the beat of silence that follows, Josh's eyes are the size of dinner plates and he gestures to the phone, miming tapping buttons and mouthing the words "put it on speaker," to which I shake my head no.

"There's a lifestyle magazine in DC. It's a pretty big deal locally and their subscriber base is an ideal advertising pool for my business. They had a last-minute cancellation and somehow found out that I'm married to a soldier. They want to do a business profile on me and my small business."

I'm processing, but slowly. "Because you're married to a soldier?"

The long exhale bathes the speaker in sound for a few seconds. "I guess. I don't know. Is that super sketchy? We should say no—I should definitely say no. Right? Obviously. And that's, yeah. I mean that's what I need to—"

"Absolutely not. This is great. Take the profile and just tell me what to do."

After a few more minutes of insisting, she gives me the details.

My smile widens bit by bit with every item of information she shares. By the time I hang up, Josh is practically pulling his hair out, desperate for me to fill in the blanks.

"She needs me." Damn, it feels good to say that out

loud. Probably makes me a jerk to think so, but I can't deny it.

"And?" Josh urges.

I make no attempt to stifle my smile. "And we'll be doing a day in the life with her. So she needs me to move in with her since we're married."

Josh grins and claps his hands together. "It's on."

No disagreement comes from me, because I feel the same. I've been racking my brain for a way to get through to her—to show her I can show up for her, that I'm not running. I need to woo her and help her and love her—do all the things I've always wanted to do but never let myself.

Now she's unwittingly served me up the perfect opportunity to do exactly that.

"It's definitely on."

CHAPTER TWENTY-SIX

Janie

Goob and Snickerdoodle greet each other like they're long-lost brothers, and a smile breaks through the rampant stress-induced resting beast face I've been rocking since I got the call from *DC Spirit Magazine: The Spirit of DC*.

And yes, that is the full title of the publication, and no, I'm not going to think about how repetitive and awful it is because it's *the* place to get a profile, not to mention the New Year shoot! I don't even know how they got my name but apparently someone on their board heard about my business through a friend and they recently found out I'm married to a soldier and wanted to celebrate that. What?

No idea how this happened. I'd suspect my parents had pulled strings but they simply wouldn't, nor do they know I'm married. It must be someone connected to Colin's work. It's wild, and it does mean the marriage will be public knowledge, but by the time my parents read it, we'll likely be on the way to divorce.

Maybe not, if he's serious...

I can't think about that. I can't. I won't. Not about my parents finding out nor about whatever happens when all of our plans are over.

There's a style consultant coming out today to review the house for where they want to shoot. This means we need to make sure it looks like Colin has been living here as my spouse for more than an hour in the next three hours.

Tomorrow, they start the shoot. Then they're coming back early the twenty-third and planning to shoot all day. *All day.* I can't imagine how many photos they want, but I'm not going to worry about it. This is a huge break for my business and it might even help my parents realize I own an actual business, not just a little project or hobby or whatever it is they're telling themselves I'm doing all day every day five to seven days a week. The caveat here is they'll have to look past the whole marriage thing which might be a tiny bit of a wrinkle in their plans for me.

Anyway.

It's not just for them. It's for me. Because what I want more than anything is to have enough of my own clientele that I can turn them down when they refer someone who clearly doesn't actually want *my* sensibility. You'd think that'd be part of the decision-making process, but I'm not naïve enough to miss the reality that many of those people are working with me to garner favor from my family.

My parents have a lot of money. My uncle is a former US senator with incredible connections and my aunt is a former circuit court judge. The Gruff family connections reach far and wide and I'm not about to underestimate that.

Therefore, I'd love to simply not be a part of the whole game.

We set up Goob's litterbox near Snickerdoodle's and nestle in a few things Colin brought. The collection of beds, toys, and a blanket he already referred to as "Goob's blanky" makes me dreadfully aware that this time is going to be absolute poison to my resolve to keep my emotional distance from him.

I was doing okay with the break—feeling stronger and determined to clear my head of all the noise and focus on taking the opportunity to put Barron off my trail at the family party, but not cave.

Not allow myself to collapse into the sweet abyss of my feelings for Colin.

Because that sleepless night before we got the cats? *Yeah.* That had clarified how underneath my desire for friendship and hesitant participation in all of this, there lay a deep, possibly endless well of feelings concerning Colin. And despite the years and years and *years* of hurt and missing him and longing, so much of it was still—*is* still, if I'm honest—love.

There's still so much love and adoration for the man just waiting to sneak through and bubble up between us. But I know very well I can't trust him. He's proven that and even acknowledged it. So.

Space.

Except next, I got this email, then a call about what a perfect fit I'd be and how, when they heard I had a military husband who'd just moved back stateside, they were just *desperate* to shoot the feature with me and Colin.

I gave myself a solid six hours to deliberate, consulted very vaguely with Andy and Grace via text, and then called him.

And here we are.

"You'll be in here. Obviously, you can go home, but I also hate for you to do that. I—" I shake my head, frazzled and not doing a great job handling it.

But before I can explain or give him outs or anything else, his palms cup my shoulders and he's catching my gaze.

"Hey. I'm fine. I'm happy to do this, and I'm not worried about the sleeping arrangements. I'd probably rather stay here, though, and I'll just take the couch, than worry about running late and setting off any alarms for the crew if they show up early tomorrow."

I heave a big breath. "Okay. Great. Thank you. I know this is a lot more than you bargained for."

I'm not sure I actually see the light in his eyes flicker at the word *bargain*, but I might. I think. Hard to say.

I get it. It both sucks and is essential to be reminded that all of this is an agreement. Yes, I heard his speech after the ball. I know he said he wants something real here. And part of me is absolutely screaming *me too me too me toooooo!*

But the part that has been burned and burned and burned before?

That girl's side-eying this whole situation.

We work together to get his clothes settled into half the closet and dresser. He brought enough to make it believable, especially because we can spin it that maybe all of his stuff hasn't arrived. I suggest this when he confirms it's not just a story, it's true.

"Since my household goods are coming from overseas, they'll be another few weeks. Usually, the main shipment takes around ninety days. I sent them early and it's not the busiest season, but yeah. I'll be happy to have a real bed."

My mouth drops open. "A real bed? What does that mean? Are you sleeping on the ground?"

"Air mattress. It's a decent one, too. I bought a new couch here and my mom had a few things she's letting me borrow until the rest arrives, but... the bed."

I mentally decide there's no chance he's sleeping on my couch. He'll take the bed, I'll take the couch, and everything will be fine. We'll fluff the pillows and no one will be the wiser that our sweet little "childhood sweethearts to grown adult married couple" story is only technically true.

After a comprehensive tour of the place, which doesn't take long since it is a townhouse in Alexandria, but is hopefully thorough enough to make it clear he's lived here for at least a few weeks, we settle in for a lightning round of question and answer because I have no idea if they're going to ask him questions, or if they'll focus solely on me and the business while including a few photos of the two of us.

At three, the guy who's checking out the space arrives to see the house. I show him around, bracing for questions about why Colin only has three suits, two of which are uniforms, or where his *stuff* is, but he has no questions. He's looking at windows and asking about afternoon light.

By three twenty-three, he's measured a few things, asked all his questions, and he's gone.

I slump into the couch, head back against the squishy down cushion behind me. "I think I may end up having a heart attack by the end of the day tomorrow if this is any indication."

"Hmm. Should we check your heart rate?"

His voice is so low and warm, I blink open to find him staring at me. He's seated close, and as soon as our gazes meet, his hand slides along the sleeve of my shirt, over the exposed skin under my collar, and two fingers gently press in at the pulse point of my neck.

I swallow, weirdly self-conscious. "Sure." It's a whisper, like if I say it too loudly, something bad will happen.

Or he'll hear the tremor in my voice and he'll know exactly how much he's affecting me.

He pulls his fingers away, and I raise my brows.

"Seems a little elevated, but you're not tachycardic."

"Oh, uh, I didn't realize you knew stuff like that."

He cracks a smile. "I had some basic medical training. Nothing fancy."

"Ah. Makes sense. And thanks. I just need to figure out how I'm going to not stress about the shoot for the next fourteen hours, and then we'll be fine." I hold my hand out to Snickerdoodle and Goob, who've both wandered out from wherever they've been since the guy arrived. Likely under my bed.

Colin's quiet for a minute as we take turns petting the cats and then he turns to me abruptly enough that Snickerdoodle jumps, then swishes his tail and saunters away.

"Sorry." He makes a face. "I was just going to say, let's get out of here. Let's go do something fun instead of sitting around here thinking about what they might ask tomorrow."

I'm exhausted from the wind-up of all this unexpected activity and proximity to him, but after settling into the idea, I agree. "Okay. Yeah, let's do it."

He beams, and it's then I realize maybe I've made a miscalculation. Especially when he winks as he stands and says, "It's a date."

CHAPTER TWENTY-SEVEN

Colin

The internet betrayed me and gave us the wrong information about a skating rink's hours, so instead of sliding around on ice skates like I know Janie would love, we're wandering around looking at Christmas lights.

"I love DC this time of year," she says, a smile in her voice I want to see.

I'm trying not to stare at her, though. I snuck in the "it's a date" and she didn't jump to correct me, but I know I'm on thin ice.

Thinner ice than I would've been on if we'd gone skating—ha.

I only have tonight and tomorrow to make this click for her, and I can't help the ticking clock in the back of my mind. So I'm trying to soak in the time, but also wow her a little.

"It's beautiful, for sure. Have you ever been to Germany at Christmastime?"

She hums. "No, but I've always wanted to. I went to Paris one year..."

We slow and I look at her under the glow of a streetlight to see why she faded off. "And?"

"The city was beautiful, of course. The person I was with," she pauses, a few tendrils of hair rustle against her cheek when the wind whips up around us.

A scorpion of jealousy stings me right in the chest. I can read what she's not saying. A guy took her to Paris. It sure wasn't me.

"Was it serious?" It's a silly question because who takes a woman to Paris he's not serious about?

She chuckles under her breath. "You'd think, right?"

I can't decipher her expression and it isn't helping that I'm nearly asphyxiating on envy of a man whose name I don't know. "Yes."

"I thought we were flying to New York to help his sister pack up and move home from college, which was weird enough considering we'd been on three dates. But then we boarded his private plane and the captain announced we were going to Paris and I almost laughed in his face."

Did I say jealousy?

Never met him.

"But you still went on the trip?" I don't imagine Janie would go along with something so easily.

She lifts one shoulder, then bites her lip. "I told him it was too much, and he insisted we go. He said he got me a separate room at the hotel because he, quote, would never assume." She widens her eyes.

I laugh because she's so damn cute, and then I pull her into me and give her a hug. "Is it bad that I like you even more knowing you went with this guy only after you established he wasn't about to bribe you into his bed?"

She pulls back, a wry smile on her lips. "Probably, but I'd feel the same way."

The evening gets better because she lets me hold her hand as we traverse the national mall and visit the national Christmas tree, then the tree in front of the White House along with all the trees for each state and Puerto Rico, and finally the tree in front of the Capitol building.

I've accepted that anything that happens here, it's because Janie lets it. And I don't want to be an idiot about it, so I'm staying quiet, asking questions and gobbling up every answer she gives me.

Slowly, steadily, we fill each other in on the lives we've led the last few years. We bridge gaps and stop to get hot chocolate with whipped cream on top—I make sure there's nothing almond milk involved because of her allergy. She gives me a side glance when I ask the vendor, but then we cradle the paper cups in our hands to warm them as we walk and it's the only time all night we aren't holding hands.

"It's pretty amazing that you were still working from your house and didn't have an office when we saw each other in Vegas, and now you've got this thriving business about to be featured in a magazine." I internally laugh at how understated "saw each other in Vegas" is compared to what really happened.

I could've more accurately said, "when I married you in Vegas like I should've done long before that," but it wouldn't sound right. Not yet.

Not until she can believe me.

"It is pretty wild. At the same time, it feels like I've been working toward it since I started college."

She shivers and I tug her closer, tucking her into my side as the night gets colder.

"I know I have no right to say it, but I'm proud of you. You've stuck to what you had in mind for yourself and you've pushed toward your dreams. I hope *you're* proud of you."

The look she gives me is so... full. I can't think of it any other way. And I can't help but interpret some of what's hiding behind her expression as hope. For what, I don't know exactly, but I think I feel the same way. Maybe this magazine shoot will be the best thing that ever could've happened to us.

"I am. Especially in the last year, I'm more focused on my vision and less on simply surviving their expectations." She huffs a self-deprecating laugh. "She says as she's scrambling to make this photoshoot work precisely because it'll show her parents her business is legitimate."

We stop under a streetlamp lighting the gravel path of the mall.

"Maybe that's part of this, but I know that's not your main driver. I don't think anyone has both success and satisfaction in their work when they're doing something to *spite* someone or something. So I know that's not you."

She nods, contemplative, and sips her hot chocolate. I do the same to keep from lecturing on all her qualities. She doesn't need me to do that right now, I don't think. She's always needed time to process, and I've always been able to give it to her.

Except when I failed her completely by leaving. Yeah. Except then.

"I'm trying to figure out whether that's true or if I just *want* it to be true. But I think it is. I want this feature to go well because I want people to be drawn to the business for me and my style and what I offer. Not to get in good with my parents."

I scoff. "Imagine that."

"Right?"

The glint in her eye and the sly smile on her mouth snaps a thread and all at once, I move. My free hand finds its home behind her hair at her nape and I lean in close, drawing her face toward me and stopping just shy of pressing her lips to mine.

I wait for one second, two. I'm giving her an out, begging her to take it if she needs it, but when she shifts onto her toes, bringing us together, I'm glad no one's walking nearby to hear the sound I make. It's not fit for public consumption.

This is nothing like the fleeting, forced contact under the mistletoe next door to Santa at the ball. That was obligatory, for show, and it'd ambushed us both. This kiss is pliant. Supple. Searing heat and endless tenderness as her chilled fingers press into the stubble at my jaw. Her every touch is heaven, and I've never been less concerned what people around me are thinking than right this minute because the only thing on my mind is how to please Janie. How does she want to be kissed and held? How can I make it better and better and better for her?

I probably would've kissed her indefinitely had another cutting burst of wind not caused us both to shudder against the bone-chilling cold and bring us back to awareness. She breaks the kiss, shivering even as she bites her swollen lip and gives me a look that darn near melts my bones.

Another cruel gust rustles her hair and blasts my face, and we take that as our sign to head home.

When we've parked and are wandering back toward her house in Alexandria a while later, outdoor Edison bulbs strung across from lamp posts to the building and every tree wound with fairy lights brighten our atmosphere.

When we reach her door, I tuck her hand behind her back to draw her close. "Thanks for going with me. It's been a long time since I've seen the DC Christmas lights."

Her warm breath freezes a few inches from her mouth when she says, "Thanks for distracting me."

I'll distract you any time.

I'll distract you all night, if you like.

Maybe she reads these thoughts flashing in my eyes because we're close, breathing the same chilled air, but she whispers, "Please."

I wish it sounded desperate but instead, it's pleading. Not begging for me to take her mouth again like I've been thinking about since the second we broke apart on the mall, but a plea for space, for not this.

The spell that fell over us the last few hours is well and truly broken. She straightens and fumbles for her keys, then steps inside, and just before she closes the door, her gaze shutters entirely and she opens it wider.

"I'm sorry. I forgot you're staying here. Come in."

I never would've imagined hating being invited into Janie's home, but here we are. I'm stepping inside with dread in my gut because I don't know what's changed, what I did wrong this time, and I know she wishes I'd go home to anywhere but here.

CHAPTER TWENTY-EIGHT

Janie

I slept a few hours. It's a Christmas miracle.

I'm embarrassed to say I didn't put up much of a fight when Colin insisted on sleeping on the couch. I'm not trying to give him whiplash, but I'm scared.

That's the ugly conclusion I've come to. I'm a chicken when it comes to him, and nights like yesterday when everything felt so good seem to flip a switch I can't ignore.

I'm riding high, enjoying the sights and sounds and scents of a wintry walk on the national mall surrounded by monuments and museums that feel like old friends, and then he's kissing me, and then it all settles into my bones and I stumble.

We came inside and he poured us both glasses of water while I checked on the cats. They were curled around each other just like we'd seen them do at Andy's, and for some stupid reason, that broke my heart even more.

When I opened my mouth to say he should sleep in my bed, he cupped my shoulders in his palms and shook his head. "Sleep, Janie. We'll get through tomorrow, we'll have fun, and it'll be amazing, and then we can talk."

Amazingly, I did. I woke this morning more rested than I have been in weeks, and I'm definitely more balanced. Am I miraculously braver and ready to throw myself into whatever is happening between me and Colin?

I wish.

When I emerge from my room, I find him in dark jeans, a long-sleeved green T-shirt, and my bright white apron. He's nudging scrambled eggs around a pan, and two bagels pop in my toaster as he turns toward me.

"Morning, CP."

He's relaxed in my space and I don't know what I expected, but it helps me calm down to see it. I had explicitly tried not to imagine what he'd be doing, how his night had gone, or what we would say to each other while we wait for the photographer and crew this morning, but now I'm disarmed.

Because he called me CP, and that reminds me of who we are to each other. Not just this fraught, tense exploration of a possible but improbable future. We're friends, too, and we have been all our lives, even if there were some long periods of radio silence.

"Morning. You've been busy." My gaze travels the kitchen to see a cutting board with what looks like fresh chives chopped up and two halves of a grapefruit nestled into small bowls. "Are we feasting for breakfast?"

He shoots me a sideways grin that makes my heart flip as he slides eggs onto two plates.

"Figured we could use a solid breakfast before things

get busy. I also plan to feed you lunch later, just a heads-up."

Good grief, he's sending all my fears scattering, along with every last brain cell. His hair is a little wet on top still, the thick, dark strands freshly washed. His shirt is just a plain T-shirt but it fits him in that way that's close enough to see he's incredibly muscular without it looking like he's busting out of the material. He's got full dark stubble now, a treat I've not witnessed since high school, because every other time I've seen him save the morning after we got married, he's been clean-shaven.

He's just so handsome, and he's made me breakfast. The fact that he's even here at all is enough to bowl me over, but this thoughtfulness may indeed do me in. It also gives me a new determination.

When he sets down the pan and spatula, I invade his space. Wrapping my arms around his warm, firm torso, I shut my eyes and savor his closeness as his arms fold around me in return.

"I know I'm confusing you. I'm sorry. I'm genuinely not trying to be cryptic or make you question your sanity."

He pulls back, his smile and eyes soft for me.

"The only sanity I question is mine in years past. The person who thought it was better to stay away from you to protect himself. The guy who was stupid enough to agree to divorcing quickly instead of trying like hell to hold onto you even if we did get married on a champagne- and tequila-fueled fantasy."

I cup his cheeks and inspect his face—this handsome, familiar face I've loved all my life. He's trying so hard, and he's not just using words. Granted, words spelling out his regrets help me know he understands why his absence was hurtful. I'm no longer stuck on that.

He's here, and he's been amazing already. He's showing up for me when this is far more than our agreement. He's not just saying what I want to hear—he's putting his promise to do better into action.

And I need to do the same. What a waste to have a man like this trying for me and not do the same? Will I ever forgive myself if I stay stuck on past hurts and don't allow myself to see what could be, especially given that we've both had time to grow and mature?

So I confess and promise, "I'm going to try, okay?"

His brown eyes flicker back and forth between mine. "Thank you."

I swallow, nerves and hope and desire welling up in me. "Thank you. For being here. And for last night—the walk and the lights and the..." My throat works to swallow again. "The kiss."

His gaze intensifies. "I should be thanking you for that, I think. But please, let me know whenever you want to do it again and I'm yours."

I grin, a touch of heat at my cheeks and an easing of pressure in my chest. If we can joke and play and flirt, maybe I can do this.

No, I can. I will.

I am.

He pulls away when the toaster pops with another bagel. "I got us bagels this morning. I hope that's okay. I was craving something hearty, and I noticed the shop when we drove the cats over the other day, so I stopped in earlier."

"Great idea. Bagel Mensch is my favorite. I have to stop myself from eating there every day."

He's busy assembling plates, then carrying them to the table, so I follow with the grapefruit.

"I don't see why you should stop yourself."

I chuckle. "Fair. Maybe my new year's resolution will be to eat there more often."

He fills a mug in front of me he must've set at the table earlier with steaming coffee, then pours some in one next to his plate. When he sits, he settles his napkin in his lap and grins.

"Good, maybe I'll join you."

I don't demur and act like I don't love the idea. I just smile, and for the first time in a long time, I don't resist the warmth accompanying an image of me and Colin eating bagels a few times a week for... ever.

CHAPTER TWENTY-NINE

Colin

Janie still looks fresh and energized after hours of interview questions and careful photos of every nook and cranny of her house.

The topics of conversation have ranged from how long she's lived here to how we met to what our Christmas plans are this year. The writer asked about our evening routine, which Janie made up on the spot.

"We love to watch TV or movies on the couch. Sometimes, we do a puzzle if we're getting wild." She grins, then with a sly smile, pulls out a contraption from a large storage drawer in her coffee table that turns out to be a puzzle board that folds up and currently contains a thousand-piece Christmas-themed puzzle. "This is what we're working on now like real heroes."

The journalist laughs and I stand there marveling at the depth of her nerdiness. There's also a keen piece of me saying, "Yes. That. I'll have all of that." Because evenings spent watching movies and puzzling with her sounds like a dream.

It is a dream.

As much as I have always wanted Janie, it hasn't always been physical. I loved her before I understood what attraction was, and even when we've been thousands of miles apart, I've simply wanted to be near her. I used to swear I could breathe easier when I'd visit my mom, despite the memories that house holds of my father, because it was close to where I'd spent so much time with Janie growing up.

I get that all of this makes my absence all the more messed up. And honestly, I know I need to complete the explanation. I need to connect the dots for her and help her understand the full picture. But so far, she seems accepting of my reasoning and the fact that I've made it very clear I regret those choices.

She's trying. She really is. She's not fake and she's not telling lies. She's using language that is either vague, or specific to *her* and just looping me in, like the puzzles. And I want every inch of the picture she paints.

"This is where we usually eat meals," she said earlier, on a tour of the house. It's obvious we'd eat at the table, but apparently, the interviewer said a lot of people she encounters eat on the couch.

I get that. Especially since I don't currently have a table in the continental United States, I tend to sit with my plate on the coffee table and eat while watching TV. The thought of sitting across from Janie and sharing all our meals, or even some of them, sounds like yet another slice of heaven.

It's the bedroom that gets me most, of course. Not only because yes, I want to have everything with Janie, but also because there's nothing more intimate to a routine than sleep. When we're asleep, we're fully vulnerable. When she says, "This is my side of the bed," I know she's saying that because it's true. The implication is that the far side is mine.

I want it. So badly.

To have a side of her bed. To have her bed be mine, her home be mine.

This wanting is nearly addling my brain I want it so much, and every smiling photo and staged light makes it all the more vivid.

Hours after they first arrived, the crew shifts to the front door. It's golden hour, early this time of year, but the buttery light is a photographer's dream, or so they tell us.

"We'll grab a few shots of you two right here on the front stoop for some socials promo," the coordinator explains, tugging at a few pine needles in Janie's fresh pine wreath that have died and tossing them behind her when she's got them all.

"Sorry. I can never seem to figure out how to keep those looking nice for as long as I probably should," Janie says, fluffing the red bow at the bottom of the wreath.

I can see the weight of the day on her now, but as soon as they ask us to pose, she's got her shoulders back and her smile ready. She's so gorgeous, I don't know why they bother having me in the shot.

"Good. And now a kiss?" the coordinator asks.

I turn to her and don't let us overthink it. I gently draw her in with a hand on her back and after a moment of eye contact to make sure she wasn't about to brush them off, press a long, slow kiss to lips.

When we release, the coordinator is fanning herself and the photographer is mumbling something.

"I hope I'm that hot for my husband after five years of

marriage," the writer muses aloud, and Janie and I share a look.

I don't know what her side of it says, but I hope she can read that for me, I don't know that I'll ever not be *hot* for her. After all, this has been my perpetual state for a solid two decades now.

Blissfully, they determine they've got what they need and they won't be back in the morning. We are nothing but grateful for this, though I'm sorry to see the excuse to stay here with her another night and another day disappear.

A few more minutes and we're shaking hands, thanking them, and shutting the door. Janie leans against it, hand on the knob, and lets her feet slide out from underneath her so she sinks to the hardwood floor.

"I am so tired."

Her eyes are drooping, and I suspect if I left her there, she might actually fall asleep.

"That lasted longer than I expected." Partly because they had equipment issues they didn't realize until more than an hour in. Partly because two of the people involved took lunch breaks at different times and didn't realize they hadn't shared whatever information they possessed in order for us to continue without them. It was one thing after another and I'm not surprised they ended up being here until the light is fading and the wintry night is settling in.

"You and me both. But it's done. We can relax now," she says then peers up at me, her arms hanging limply by her sides.

I planned to pull her up by her hands, but I bypass that route and crouch low, hauling her over my shoulder and standing.

"Colin! What are you doing? You can't hold me like this!" She's more awake now that she's hanging over my shoulder, her back arched so her head is up, but I'm more than halfway to the couch.

"Seems like I can."

She swats at my butt and I gasp in surprise.

"You just spanked me?" I flip her over onto the couch, then brace myself over her. "Really, CP?"

She's red-faced and grinning. "That's what you get for manhandling me, ya butthead."

I chuckle. "Butthead. Now, now, now, Ms. Gruff. We can't have language like that. This is a family establishment."

She sniffs and raises a shoulder, which happens to be bare since the slouchy sweater she's wearing slid down to reveal a delicious section of her collar bone, shoulder, and upper arm. I drag the pad of one finger along the delicate wing of her decolletage.

My voice is low and a little rough. "You were brilliant today."

"Thank you. Truly, thank you for being here and doing all this."

She swallows, the beautiful lines of her throat drawing my eye. It takes all my concentration not to press my lips there, to leave a mark. Not surprisingly, spending the day hearing her refer to me as her husband has weakened my resolve to keep my distance and give her space.

But I'm determined to give her whatever she needs, and right now, she's exhausted and I shouldn't be indulging in the many desires running rampant in my head, so I push off the couch to stand.

She bolts upright.

"I should head out. Let you get some rest. I'll be back for Goob tomorrow," I pledge, knowing I need to get out of here before my willpower flags any more than it already has.

"Wait, why?"

She reaches for me but I'm already edging back, slipping my hands into my pockets to force control.

"Seriously, is something wrong?"

She's standing and there's, crap, there's hurt in her voice. I rush back toward her, hands grasping hers.

"Sorry. I'm sorry. You're exhausted. I am, too. It's been a long day and they're not coming tomorrow anymore so I thought I'd get out of your hair. Give you space."

She dips her chin and whispers, "Okay," and it's like we tunnel back into the past. I know what this is because I've seen it before.

"Wait, do you want me to stay?"

CHAPTER THIRTY

Janie

The embarrassment that snuck in when he nearly jumped out of his skin to get away from me melts at the look in his eyes—at the disbelief and hope in his tone.

I grab him by the collar of his shirt and pull him closer. "Yes. I want you to stay and have dinner and watch a movie. Maybe work on a puzzle, if you're that kind of guy."

"I can be that kind of guy."

He says this immediately, his hands settling on my waist.

My stomach flips and swoops low. The more we touch, the more I want the contact. After today, after how supportive he's been, I can't seem to want anything but more time with him.

I grin. "Good. Then you go decide what we watch while I get the menus."

Ten minutes later, we've placed our order for delivery

dinner and we're settled on the couch as the beginning notes of *The Holiday* start up.

"What's the longest relationship you've had?"

It could be the glass of red wine I've already had half of, but not likely. I may have an empty stomach, but I think this boldness to know more about his life stems from the knowledge that there's no hope for us if we can't talk about the hard things. We've now spent more than half of our lives avoiding being honest.

Today's shoot was draining on several levels, but the result that came out of it for me was twofold. First, I want this to light a fire in my business. I'm hopeful it'll bring business to Andy's Place, too, since we had a full discussion about adopting Goob and Snickerdoodle.

The growth won't only come from this, of course, because it's so rarely one thing that gets businesses moving, but since my design firm primarily works locally, this could genuinely make a big difference in my clientele.

Second, I had a day to imagine a life with Colin. Not dream it, but imagine the details about where we'd eat our meals and what we do at night. His toothbrush is already in my bathroom, his glasses are on the nightstand opposite mine. It's silly such small details should impact me, but they have.

They are.

And now, I want to know it all so I can see...

"I dated someone on and off for a year, but in that time, we were long-distance for most of it." He squints at the TV. "Honestly, that was far and away the longest I ever had or even attempted."

I *hmm* and wonder if it makes me petty that I'm both happy and sad this is the case. Skipping that for now, I tell him, "Same for me. I mean, not the long-distance part, but... a year. And it was about a decade ago, now."

In fact, the only reason I ever went out with the guy was because I'd heard Colin was home for Christmas and for some insane reason, I thought maybe he'd visit me. I'd graduated college the summer prior and was interning with a designer in Boston. Something about both of us traveling home to Virginia made it seem like we were there for each other.

Of course he didn't.

It'd given me the shove I needed to say yes to a guy who'd asked me out once or twice. I said yes. He was nice and in the end, that was all it was. When time came for me to move on from that internship and look at broadening my experience, I left Boston, and him.

"What's wrong with us, do you think?" His half smile doesn't hide the question's genuine root. He's not just joking.

I have to weigh my answer because I'm done pretending, yes, but that doesn't mean I'm ready to tell him I think it's because we've been waiting on each other. That I measured every man I met against him and they all came up lacking, even when he'd left me alone for years. That my heart was too broken over him to get fixed for anyone else.

That last thought is bittersweet because something I'm beginning to realize is that my heart might be whole again. Sometime after I thought our divorce would've been finalized, I'd put to bed what I'd thought was foolish hope over him. Granted, it came roaring back to life the second I heard from him, but it was more cautious. Measured. Not so willing to fling itself against the glass.

No, I won't say all that right now. "I don't know. I don't

think it means we're messed up, but maybe it means we just haven't met the right people yet."

His gaze finds mine and does that thing where he shifts between my eyes, searching. His lips part and he's slow to bring out the words, but when he does, I'm left speechless and a little buzzed, but it can't be from my still-half-full glass of wine.

"I had already found the right person. I just kept messing it up."

The doorbell rings. Our food's here.

"I'll grab it," he says and jumps up, so I do, too. Because what can I say to that?

Dinner helps loosen the knot we tied before it arrived, and we sit on the couch, flouting all of the claims about sitting at the table.

"We sounded so cultured, sitting at the table night after night. Did imaginary us light candles, too?" he asks, then takes a huge bite of naan.

"Absolutely. We're very fancy. Placemats and napkin rings kind of people for sure." I like that we're poking fun, though I wonder if it bothers him that I lied. "I hope I didn't say anything that made you uncomfortable. I tried to mostly talk about myself."

"You were brilliant. I noticed how you'd say something true about what you do and it left the author free to interpret what I'd do, too. My guess is she assumed I did the same or something like that. You avoided lying except when absolutely necessary and you didn't lie about anything that mattered."

I tsk. "I don't know. Lying about being married is pretty bad." I can't seem to summon any guilt about it, though.

He finishes chewing a bite, then grins. "Ah, but we *are* actually married. So that's not a lie."

"True, sure. So I guess the real lie is that we're married and together? Cohabitating?" What an odd thing to specify.

"Exactly. And in the military world, couples live apart for all kinds of reasons. They call it 'geobaching.'"

I am mildly horrified. "Ew, like you're in a different zip code so you're suddenly a bachelor? Is that like some underground military open marriage thing?"

He chuckles. "No, nothing so sinister. It just means the soldier goes to whatever assignment—sometimes overseas, but sometimes stateside in a place where schools don't work. Or maybe the spouse is getting a degree and can't move, or has a great job, or needs to care for family—whatever. So the servicemember moves and the family or spouse stays put. It's not at all uncommon."

Less horrifying, thankfully. "So in your military context, the story is that you were geobaching so I could stay here near family."

His brows crease. "And for your business. You've built something great here, so that's not hard to believe. Military spouses are often un- or under-employed, and finding work is already hard enough, let alone picking up and doing it every two to three years. You have an established business, you're building your name. It's not unreasonable at all to believe that we would've wanted you to continue pursuing your dream even while I'm active duty."

Jack Black is charming Kate Winslet on screen, and we turn our attention to the movie for a few minutes, though my mind is busy sorting through all he said.

I end up verbalizing my question instead of keeping it inside. It's audacious, maybe, but I can't pretend my mind isn't reeling with the idea that we'd live apart if we were really married.

"So, sorry, I just need to clarify. If we, uh, really did this.

If we were married and stayed that way, or whatever, you know—"

"Yes, Janie. I get it. I've already said..."

I nod. "So yeah, would we live apart?"

His brows raise. "Would you want to?"

"No, I'm asking you."

He holds my gaze, intense and focused, then his hand comes to cradle my face. "If we did this—stayed married, if you were my wife, Janie, I wouldn't want to be parted from you. Not ever."

I pull in a shaky breath and nod once more, bursts of longing and joy and a healthy amount of disbelief that he just said those words straight to my face bounding around in my chest.

"And you? Would you want to stay together?"

He means in this scenario where we're knowingly married, choosing it.

He's being so honest with me, I meet him right there, if not quite so brave. "People live all over the world, and they should have beautiful spaces wherever they are."

He understands me, I think, because his beautiful mouth spreads into a pleased smile. "Yeah?"

"Yeah."

And then we're just sitting there watching the movie, grinning as though it's Jack Black singing through movie scores that has us so happy and not this truth we've both settled on.

The question is, will it matter?

CHAPTER THIRTY-ONE

Colin

I wake up sprawled on Janie's couch, a thousand-pound weight on my chest, my head on fire with heat surrounding me, and what I think is Janie tucked under my arm that is currently completely numb.

As I blink the world into existence through dried-out contacts, I see the orange furball sitting on my chest, staring at me like the subtle movement and groan that emerged from me were rather an inconvenience for him.

"Sorry, Goob," I mutter, then reach up with my free hand to figure out the head situation. I'm met with the high-speed purr of Snickerdoodle, who has taken up residence curled around my head like the softest, hottest little hat ever.

I debate staying put, but my arm is numb, my body is rapidly overheating, and even though I want Janie to get more sleep, I can't stay here. I shift and Goob stands, spearing me with his weight now focused into sharp points in my chest, and Snickerdoodle goes, too.

Janie's head pops up, and when she tries to look back at me, because of the way she's snuggled under one arm, she rolls away just a touch. I'm already smiling, but seeing her has me so happy, my face isn't even awake enough to grin so wide.

Except her expression changes and in a flash, there's a thunk and she's no longer next to me. My useless, numb arm did nothing when she toppled off the couch and onto the floor.

"Are you okay?" I scramble up, horrified.

She's already giggling, though. "I am beauty and grace. Wow."

"That must've hurt. Are you alright?"

I don't know why I'm mildly panicked, but it must have to do with the bliss of being close to her and then the sudden sense she was in danger. Or maybe it's the odd sensation that because we slept next to each other on the couch, now she's hurt?

Or my tired brain isn't functioning. I kneel next to her on the rug and watch her grimace as she rubs at her hip.

"That's going to make a pretty bruise, I bet."

She laughs again, and a touch of relief hits me.

We're fine. She's fine.

She shifts slowly, moving in a way that shows me the impact did hurt, and I help her back onto the couch. Snickerdoodle has arrived to sniff around and see what all the hubbub was about.

"Ice? Heating pad?" My gaze shoots to where her hands moves over her hip and around to the backside of her sweatpants where she must've taken the brunt of the fall. Heroically, I bounce my eyes away but say, "Massage?"

She swats at me and laughs. "No. I'll survive. Thank you."

Hand to my heart, I give her a sincere look. "I will make the sacrifice if you need it."

She rolls her eyes, but we both know I'm joking.

Well, at least about this. Do I want to touch her? For sure. No doubt. But I'm purposefully being a creeper to make her laugh now.

She's still smiling as she says, "So, we slept on the couch."

I nod, something fizzy in my chest. "We did. And while I'll say it was fine the first night, I didn't love the double occupancy."

"Yeah, I will agree with that. Next time, we move to the bed. Agreed?"

Her gaze shifts up to mine, those blue eyes wide and clear.

Did my heart stop? Or am I still asleep on this couch, imagining all of this?

Did Janie just invite me into her bed?

It's not that deep. I know it's not. She's not saying sleep with her like, finally consummate our marriage. She's saying sleep like we just did. And since I'm not functioning on all cylinders just yet, I blurt that out.

Merry Christmas to me, even so.

"Yeah, to sleep. Count sheep. Catch some z's." I immediately want to erase everything that just came out of my mouth.

She blinks, a befuddled little line creasing her forehead. "Yeah, um, okay. I need coffee."

Thank goodness. "Same. Obviously."

An hour later, we've both properly caffeinated and cleaned up, and my mom has been pinging me with texts about every six minutes. She's worn me down enough that when Janie emerges from her room in a pair of jeans and a bright red sweater, I don't let the possibilities pile up. I just ask.

"Do you have plans today?" We were supposed to be doing the shoot again today, so now it feels like there's a gap in our schedule and I'm not sure how to fill it.

"Do you? I figured you might need to pop into work, but I'm free." She smiles like saying it out loud is a relief. "I'm genuinely so glad I took an actual Christmas break this year."

"Proud of you," I say, impulsively reaching out and brushing my thumb over the apple of her cheek.

She's so beautiful, it makes me stupid. I should be keeping my hands to myself. Sure, we slept wrapped up in each other, but we didn't even kiss again last night. I know what I want and it sure sounds like Janie's getting there, but until she knows, I'm not going to push. I'm not going to take.

Except maybe the occasional point of contact because when you love a girl for going on two decades, signs occasionally break loose.

"Thanks," she says, her smile soft.

"And hey, for the record, I'm not going into work again until after New Year's." I'd decided yesterday, sometime around the second time she called me her husband.

Now her smile widens into a beaming grin. "Now it's my turn to say *I'm* proud of *you*."

Then she steps right into my space and hugs me. So easily. Like the distance my garbage cowardice and endless angst brought us for years has been erased.

The hope I've cradled in my chest for so long doubles in size. It's gotten bigger every time I've seen her, touched her, talked to her, listened to her, but this? It might just burst out of me. I ease back, settling my hands at her waist again. It's oddly intimate, but since she's still got her hands on my shoulders, it feels natural.

"I've got to drop off presents for my mom and sisters. Do you want to come with me?" There was probably a smoother way to invite her, but I've never had moves with this woman. I want her in my family's space on Christmas Eve, and I don't know how to maneuver that in any subtle way except to ask.

"Do you think they'd—"

"I *know* they'd love to see you."

And they will.

The only question is how it'll feel being with them since they know the truth.

CHAPTER THIRTY-TWO

Janie

Mrs. Vicente hugs me so tight I feel like I might pop. Colin insisted we get dinner before going over or we'd have to stay for a meal at his family's house and he didn't seem to want that. Our lazy day of reading, watching Christmas movies, and playing with the cats flew by and now, here we are. Out of our bubble.

I make a point to *not* assume it's because he doesn't want me with them for long. I'm honestly surprised he invited me to go with him. He rarely invited me over when we were younger. The only times I visited were when he knew everyone else would be gone, and the handful of times I showed up without an invitation.

This family felt so different from mine. Even now, Lina's hugging me, Bianca's cuddling a snoozing baby, two toddlers are making the sounds a feral cat would and clinging to Colin's legs, and the man I assume is Bianca's husband is clapping Colin on the back, then drawing him in for a hug even with his children Velcroed on. It's so much lively affection, so much warmth, it's completely unfamiliar except that I've caught glimpses of it elsewhere. A friend's house, or between Andy and Will.

"We're not staying long. Just wanted to drop off presents," Colin announces, because he's barely gotten a word in since we walked in the door.

Great upheaval comes from the floor, where one little girl flops back onto the ground and begins to mean-mug Colin while the other chants, "No, no, no!"

"Oh, come on. You have to eat something, at least." Mrs. Vicente stands like she's going to cook something, but Colin catches her up into another hug.

"Thanks, Mom, but I took Janie out for a little date night right before this."

He chose his words wisely. There wouldn't have been anything else to distract his mother like those words, and the sly smile that spreads across her mouth and consumes her entire demeanor is telling, for sure.

"Oh, did you?" Her eyes are downright sparkling. "How nice."

Colin's eyes catch mine and we share a look. We talked on the way over about how everyone here knew we'd gotten married in Vegas, had planned to divorce and move on like it never happened, but now...

Well, we didn't name what *now* is, but we acknowledged it's not all fake, even in the context of choosing to *appear* married for both his work and my family—and of course the magazine feature.

It all felt a little murky and yet not sitting down across from each other like we're negotiating a settlement made sense. We weren't naming what this is because it's not easy to label. We're in the middle of something, not at the destination.

"So how's it going? With your work and everything?"

This comes from Lina, who's shifting her attention between me and Colin. Speaking of, he brings me a mug with a giant Grinch face on it and murmurs, "Careful, it's hot."

I smile up at him and he touches the edge of his Cindy Lou Who mug to mine in a toast.

Is it adorable that he brought me hot chocolate without me asking? Yes. Is it also adorable that he gave me the Grinch mug? Another yes, especially if he did it because he remembers how much I loved the original Grinch book as a kid.

"Thank you," I say, looking up at him where he's standing next to my chair.

He tucks some hair behind my ear. "Of course."

"Um, okay. That answered perfectly."

Colin and I both look at Lina to find a Cheshire smile on her face. She's utterly delighted by what she witnessed. But what did she?

I suppose our interaction had been rather couple-like. She hasn't seen us together since we were in high school, so it probably looked totally natural.

Funny thing is, it *is* natural. When I get out of my head long enough to stop second-guessing everything that *could* happen, being with Colin is as simple as existing.

"They do look good together," Bianca's husband is saying, right as Bianca smiles down at the baby in her arms, then back up at her husband to say, "They always have."

The two older kids race toward their mom, but their dad intercepts them, swinging them up into his arms with a growly, fun dad-sound I am certain my father never uttered. I wonder if Colin's did, either.

Mrs. Vicente is taking it all in, watching her daughters and son-in-law cast votes for our situation without trying to soften them or make either of us comfortable.

Colin's hand slides to my shoulder and squeezes gently. It's a show of solidarity, comfort, and maybe a reminder that what they say doesn't determine anything for us. We do that.

Lina groans dramatically. "You guys are adorable. Can we just get past this whole 'Mom didn't send in the paperwork' thing and you can just stay married and live happily ever after?"

"Are you gonna make a baby now, Uncle Colin?" Bianca's oldest girl asks, her tiny voice so precious it takes me a second to register.

Colin makes a sound not unlike a startled gurgle and Lina instantly points and laughs. My cheeks heat, but I chuckle and cover my mouth because I'm leaving that one to Uncle Colin.

"Well, everyone, I think that's our cue," Colin says, and sets his mug on the table next to mine.

Everyone chuckles and I admire the bright red hue of Colin's cheeks. He's adorable, and somehow this makes me want to say yes to the little girl all the more.

"No, no, no. We're not running you off, and we won't keep commenting. Stay and finish your hot chocolate. Play a game or two. Then you can go and know you've spent time with your family on Christmas Eve at your childhood home just like your mother always dreams each year."

I chuckle into my mug, and Colin voices my thoughts.

"Wow, guilt trip, huh? Going for the low blows?" But he

pulls his mom into another quick hug. "If Janie's up for the madness, then we'll stay."

Everyone's eyes shift to mine and wait.

"Oh, great, no pressure, huh?" I joke, then grin as Colin laughs and Lina's face betrays her delight.

We do stay. We end up hanging around until nearly eleven o'clock that night, far longer than we intended when Colin said we'd be "in and out within an hour" before dinner. But anytime he checks on me, I make sure he knows I'm comfortable.

His family is captivating. His nieces pass out on the couch not long after their dad gets them dressed in matching Christmas jammies and something about their innocent exhaustion makes my heart squeeze.

I cannot shake what his mom said. It's not just me he's been away from. I know he's stayed in touch and I gathered each of the girls has visited him overseas when he was in Germany and not deployed, but it drills home that his absence hasn't just been about me.

And goodness, that sounds awfully self-centered, but it's taken me until now to really understand that part of his being gone has been a reality of his service. He's lived apart from his wonderful, warm, loving family for so long, and I know that's even harder on everyone with Mr. Vicente out of the picture.

Granted, the reality that their dad isn't here doesn't seem to haunt anyone as much as it does Colin and I only know this because of his periodic mentions of it. I'm not sure how much it affects him now, but he certainly isn't sitting in his mother's living room wishing his father were here.

We say our goodbyes and I receive quality hugs from

every member of the Vicente family. It's beautiful. They're the most lovely people and I've always thought so.

I'm reflecting on this in the car when Colin pulls up to the house. He opens my door, then waits patiently as I key us inside and the kitties greet us as though we abandoned them for days and not a matter of about six hours.

After we've petted and reassured them they haven't, in fact, been left for dead, we settle in on the couch without discussion. We both simply know that's where we're heading.

"Sorry that turned into a thing." He runs a hand through his hair, gaze on the fireplace where I turned on a low flame.

"I loved it. Thank you for taking me with you."

When his eyes meet mine, it feels like there's so much more than the flicker of firelight there. My chest feels full and my heart is thrumming. He doesn't speak and I'm not sure what I want him to say, what I need him to say, but when he laces our fingers together, it feels like an answer.

"My mom has always loved you." His voice is low and rumbly after hours of talking and laughing. His attention is fixed on our hands, and with his free one, he touches the bright red of each of my painted fingernails.

"I've always loved her. I was thinking that on the way home—how much I've always liked them."

He breathes so quietly, and I can't help asking the question niggling at me.

"Why didn't you want me around them when we were growing up?"

His gaze snaps to mine. "What?"

"You never invited me over. I only ever saw your house when it was empty with a handful of exceptions, and it was always because your mom surprised you or she'd see me and insist I come to dinner."

He struggles, jaw moving and lips parting for a second before he actually speaks. "I was embarrassed. Not of them—not my sisters and my mom, obviously, but my dad…" He shakes his head. "And then after he went to jail, I was so used to keeping that part of my life separate from us."

"I get that." I learned the lesson at intervals, but never without heartache. My parents made sure I knew they didn't approve of my friendship with Colin, then that I couldn't take him to prom, and so on. So I didn't tell them how much I saw him or cared about him, and certainly never that I loved him. Not that I would've told them such a thing anyway.

The party will be the first time they see Colin since he left for the military academy and I don't want to think about it. I don't care if they approve of him anymore, that's for sure, but I just don't want to break this happiness and ease between us with those invading thoughts.

Instead, I stand and tug on his hand. When his brow furrows, I pull more insistently until he stands and I say, "Let's go to bed."

CHAPTER THIRTY-THREE

Colin

She doesn't wait for me to respond. Instead, she tows me along behind her and I follow like a good little boat to her dinghy. I'll go wherever she takes me. *Aye aye, Captain.*

Wrong branch of service, of course, but I'm helpless against her.

"You, uh, I, should, uh—"

Her hand squeezes mine. It should reassure me, but all it does is scramble my brain a little more until we reach the frame of her door and I blurt out, "I can take the couch."

She turns slowly, completely poised even in the face of my outburst.

"Do you want to take the couch?" Her gaze softens when she looks at me, likely reading the confusion and tension in my face. "I mean we should sleep. I'd like to be a little more settled before we take any major steps physically, but after spending the night on the couch last night, I think we both deserve a bed. Since my guest room is an office, and since I trust you, I think we should go to bed and get a really good sleep so we are prepared for t-tomorrow."

That little slip over the last word is the only hint she's got nerves. I don't think they have to do with me in her bed so much as the looming party at her parents' house. And she strategically chose not to reference that even though we know it's coming, so I follow her lead.

Except I don't, because what comes out is, "You trust me?"

I know she does in some way, but fundamentally, what I'm working to rebuild is her trust in me. Sharing a bed certainly indicates a level of trust we haven't had before, and I have to make sure I'm not taking any of this the wrong way.

She brings our joined hands up and presses a kiss to the back of my hand. Her lips on my skin will never not send a thrill through me, and they do just that now.

"I do trust you. I realized tonight that some of what felt like you choosing to be out of my life was also the reality of you being in the Army. And that sounds so self-centered and honestly, it is, but being with your family, seeing how much they've missed having you here during the holidays drove it home."

"You weren't wrong, though. I made choices. I could've called, or stayed in touch. Emailed at least. I could've answered your letters."

That one shamed me the most—the way I'd read and absolutely savored every single contact she gave me—a handful of letters my freshman year at school, a few texts, and occasionally across the years, an email. It was always something simple, something to say, "I'm thinking about you and I hope you're safe," and it never failed to crush me and put me back together again.

"I know. But you've apologized. And I don't want to keep digging that up because it's done. And if what you're saying is true, you don't plan to disappear on me again." She gives me a pointed look.

I pull her in and capture her mouth. I intend for it to be a simple peck, but her hands lock around my neck in a flash and the intensity notches up. She opens for me and our bodies press tight. My hands are in her hair and at her hip, and she's kissing me back with everything she's got.

She breaks away with a laugh and exudes joy when she looks at me with kiss-stung lips. "I take that as a no, you're not going to disappear?"

I drop my forehead to hers. "No, ma'am."

The cats brush against our legs and we untangle, then go about getting ready for bed. Sliding between the sheets next to her is surreal and, not going to lie, a bit of a dream. But then, once the buzz of adrenaline evens out and I remind myself nothing is happening in this bed because we're tired and figuring things out, I settle into it. I scroll through articles from the day's news like I always do while she swipes pages in her ereader every few minutes.

The truest pleasure comes when we turn off the lights and her hand brushes over my shoulder.

"Night, Colin," she whispers, as though the dark requires it.

"Sweet dreams, CP," I say, pressing a kiss to her palm.

And then, we sleep.

Waking up is disorienting at first, but only because yet again, I'm held down by the exponential weight of Goob on my chest and Snickerdoodle inexplicably wrapped around my head. I'm debating how to extricate myself when I hear a soft giggle and look over to see Janie snapping a photo of me quite literally covered in cats.

We're not nested together; we're not wrapped up like we migrated toward one another in the night. No, we're clearly people unused to sharing a bed who kept to our sides and the only interlopers are the felines. But waking up to her laughter is one of the best things I've ever experienced, so I can't regret that my sleeping subconscious didn't bring us closer.

"Merry Christmas."

She's honestly dazzling right now as she grins and gives Snickerdoodle a little head bump as he passes by now that I've disturbed him by moving.

"Merry Christmas. And thanks for letting me stay in the bed. Couch is nice, but this is better." Goob still hasn't decided whether he's staying or going, though he's purring loudly enough I think he's determined to stay.

"I'm glad." Her hand skates over Goob's back and his purr gets even more aggressive. For an old man, he's still got an impressive little motor.

"I'm going to get the coffee started and then it's time for presents." She bounces a little, excitement in her gaze, then scoots off the bed.

I'd like to say I didn't enjoy the way her bright red shorts say *Jolly* across the backside, but then I'd be lying. And generally, I prefer honesty.

So in that spirit, let me say that my wife's shorts made *me* jolly.

Anyway.

In another hour, we're back on the couch, bellies full of coffee and cinnamon rolls she had delivered at some point yesterday and heated in the oven, and we've started a Christmas movie marathon along with a puzzle.

But I'm antsy.

My knee is bouncing and between Clark Griswold's hijinks, she slaps her hand down on my thigh to steady it.

"What's with the bouncing? Are you nervous for tonight?" She's inspecting me as though there'll be an outward tell for what's eating at me.

"Honestly? Not really." I probably should be, but I'm almost looking forward to being the man on her arm and making her unavailable to a man named Barron Banks.

"Lucky you," she says on a sigh.

I should be more sensitive to the fact that she's nervous. Of course she is. Her family has always been difficult, and showing up with me isn't going to make them happy.

Instead of letting myself obsess over my reasons for nervousness, I go for it. I hop up and jog to her room where I unearth my suitcase from her closet and find the small box in a zipped compartment. When I return, she's still seated on the couch watching me.

I sit, then open my hand to show her the box. She blinks, not understanding, so I open it and take out the small gold ring. Wonder what she did with the one we got in Vegas, but then again, it was a cheap trinket we got from the chapel's store. It didn't mean anything—not like this ring I'm holding now.

"This has been in my family for a long time. It's maybe not quite your style, but I wanted you to have a ring for tonight. If you want. No pressure, of course, but it felt like we should probably have rings and I didn't feel like it was something people would notice at a work function, but with your people..."

I trail off because she's frowning down at the little ring, but then she holds out her finger. I did get it sized, so when it slips on perfectly, I'm not surprised. But she is. Her eyes shine as she shakes her head.

"This was really thoughtful. Thank you. I'll return it."

I shake my head now. "I'm not worried about that." Mostly because I hope she won't return it. I hope she'll keep it and wear it and be mine. Or if not this one, then another we pick out together.

I know now and more with every second that I want Janie as my wife forever. Tipsy, foolish Colin of five years ago was an honest to God genius for marrying her, and I'm just sorry I didn't figure out a way to make it work the morning we woke up and realized what we'd done.

But then, she slips the ring off and slides it on her other hand. It's no longer a wedding ring. Just something non-committal.

"Sorry, I just remembered. I'm not planning on telling them we're married. It'll just be messier and more unpleasant for both of us, so for tonight, we'll just be in a serious relationship, if that's okay."

Right. I remember. Of course I remember that was always the plan.

It shouldn't matter to me, but as we settle back into puzzling and watching the movie, a pit forms in my stomach.

Mothers Of Military Network Message board:

Vic: I'm not going to say that things are looking up, but things are looking up!!!

SCLDG: Details—go!

JusticeLVR: Tell us!

CoolyKay: Edge of my seat here, friend!

Vic: They came over. They are precious. I can see it so clearly. I just need them to see it. I think they're getting closer.

CoolyKay: Adorable! I hope they will.

JusticeLVR: I'm so happy you got to spend time with them. How long has it been since he was home for Christmas?

Vic: Years. We went to him a few times, but years and years.

SCLDG: A nice gift for you then.

Vic: Yes. And thanks for whatever you did to get the story in *DC Spirit*.

JusticeLVR: She's a miracle worker! Especially if they have a little Christmas miracle love fest?

CoolyKay: Love it. Yes.

SCLDG: Another version of me would be horrified that I'm friends with someone who would write the phrase "Christmas miracle love fest," but the mother who did my level best to get my son happily married off gets it.

JusticeLVR: Haha. You're a fake Grinch, sorry to tell you.

Vic: I've spent a lot of years hating Christmas, honestly. Losing faith that my son, especially, could ever be happy. This just feels...

JusticeLVR: Hopeful?

CoolyKay: Like a beginning?

Vic: Both. It's filling me with hope. It's a lovely feeling.

SCLDG: Happy for you.

JusticeLVR: Truly.

CoolyKay: Happy and a little envious, but mostly so happy for you, Vic.

Vic: Thanks, all. More soon. And **@CoolyKay**, last to go but we won't forget!

CoolyKay: Thanks. My stubborn-as-a-mule son doesn't give me much hope, but I'm living for your updates, my friend.

CHAPTER THIRTY-FOUR

Janie

Colin's quiet as we drive to my parents' house. I'm not sure if he's more nervous than he let on earlier, or he just knows I am and can't wait to get this over with.

I've been irritated with myself all day but trying to hide it. I think I've done okay. But the feeble excuse for bravery I'm sporting now isn't going to cut it once I get in a room with Gregory and Colleen Gruff.

The slight weight of Colin's ring on my right ring finger could make me cry if I think about it hard enough. Giving this to me is such a sweet, lovely gesture, and honestly, it's a dream come true. Everything about the way he's acting is. Shifting it from my left to my right hand was almost painful, as was that flash of disappointment in his eyes. The one we got in Vegas stayed in Vegas. I left it on the bedside table, closing the door on it and the implications of it as though leaving it there meant the marriage would be left behind too.

What a hilariously naïve idea, but I can't blame myself.

All of it's got me second-guessing this plan. Should we just tell them we're married? Maybe I can say something like, "Merry Christmas, Mom and Dad. I got you a son-in-law. Surprise!"

The thought of springing this on them tonight when all of their friends will be there fills me with dread. They won't like the news for several reasons, but they would absolutely hate if I told them at a time they can't do damage control. And that's how they'll see this.

They'd see anyone I marry who isn't someone they choose that way, though, so it's not a reflection on Colin. If anything, their disapproval signals how good he is. How real.

By the time we pull up into the long, cobblestone drive and hand off the keys to a valet stationed at the front in charge of parking for the evening, my adrenaline is absolutely racing through my veins. To think that barely twenty-four hours ago, I was on the other, farthest side of the property's fence, at the Vicente home. It's a different world there—all that warmth and love in their home, and all this here.

"Hey, come here for a sec." Colin takes my hand and pulls me to the side of the house so we're tucked away for a moment. "You okay?"

I swallow and nod, but my throat is dry and my mouth is full of cotton. If it didn't dawn on me how far apart the worlds we grew up in are before, it does now. But that's not helping the present issue. "Yeah."

He huffs a laugh. "Convincing."

I exhale long and slow. "Sorry. I'm second-guessing this whole thing. Maybe we should just go?"

My supplication does nothing, as evidenced by his head shaking and the way he cups my clasped hands.

"We'll be fine. And if for a second you're over it, we'll leave. But let's go do what you wanted—get them off your back with the whole Barron thing, and give yourself some freedom."

A scream is lodged in my throat. I think about letting it out—just shrieking right here at the edge of the party and then running down the drive to find my car. Instead, I take another breath, willing calm and confidence to come to me. *Any second now.*

"You are an amazing woman. You have a successful business and good friends. You have a beautiful home and an awesome cat and, if I may say, a decent 'boyfriend.'"

He uses air quotes and it makes me wish we did have a title. Is he my actual boyfriend? Is he my husband? Is there a name for the no-man's-land between the two?

"Thank you. And you..." I don't know how to tell him how much his support and encouragement mean to me. "I'm so glad you're here with me."

"Is that my girl Janie Gruff, and who's this?"

My stomach plummets because I know that voice and I hadn't planned on him being the first one we talked to.

I catch Colin's eye and give him a look, but I guarantee he already knows who it is.

"Hi, Barron," I say, summoning a polite smile.

He's frowning, almost *aghast* at Colin's hand around my waist. Colin, though, is completely unaffected. His hand is splayed over my hip and since he's holding my long wool coat after I completely overheated on the drive, it's clear to see from any vantage point. He extends his hand to Barron.

"Colin Vicente. You are?"

Barron sneers down at his hand, but accepts it. "Barron Banks. Janie and I—"

"Oh, that's right. She mentioned you'd gone out a time or two. Is that right, love?"

He looks at me, all adoration in his eyes, but I see the wicked glint.

Okay, Colin came to play tonight, and he's not letting Barron off the hook. *Excellent.*

"It is. How are you, Barron? Did you bring someone tonight?"

It might be a low blow since I know for a fact he assumed he'd be meeting me here. The real question is *why* he assumed I'd be available to him at his beck and call since I have given him absolutely no reason to hope for such a thing.

Alas. Not all men, of course, but some of them, yes, indeed.

"I—I, yes, she'll just be a little late. She's at another party first." He raises his brows and leans in. "It's full of celebrities and that kind of thing. I would've joined her, but you know how Mother and Father are." He rolls his eyes.

Yes. I do know how they are. They insist on coming to my family's party because my uncle and aunt, the former senator and judge, will make an appearance at some point this evening. It would be pathetic to acknowledge if it weren't the way so many people functioned.

"Well, good for you. I'm going to get Janie inside before we both freeze." Colin thwacks Barron on the back and ushers me forward in the crook of his arm.

After handing off our coats to the coat check—and yes, this party has a coat check at the door—we finally share a look. I smile and he winks.

"That work okay?" he asks under his breath.

"Absolutely. He rolled with it better than expected." I'm a little impressed, actually. But thankfully, this means one down.

I'll likely need to tell Chip the truth, but otherwise, it's mostly just an evening of small talk and a quick chat with my parents to tell them I'm in a serious relationship with a boy they always hated who has turned out to be an excellent man and whom I'm very likely in love with and, oh, also am married to, but never mind about that little detail.

Easy!

We head toward the music and I scan for Chip. He and I aren't the kind to share secrets, but I'd like to be honest with him so I'm lying to one fewer person, and I need to get it over with before we deal with my parents. It'll be a little warm-up, except we'll tell him something true and them something that is a shade of the truth.

"Cocktail?" A twenty-something man in a uniform of black and white holds a tray of identical-looking highball glasses with rims salted or sugared with something red and cranberries floating around the sides. "Cranberry Crush Margarita, or my colleague has a Christmas Royale available."

Somehow, I manage not to roll my eyes and we each accept a margarita, though I know very well neither of us is about to over-imbibe. Maybe at someone else's house, I'd be charmed by the evening's signature cocktails. I'd even want to drink them. But tonight, every bit of this show is popcorn between my teeth.

Christmas music comes from a stage where a five-piece band and singer are set up. It's lovely. The house looks fantastic, if even more scrubbed of personality with so many people and waitstaff in attendance. A giant live Christmas tree with lavish gold and silver decorations towers over the room.

I hear Chip's weird laugh right when Colin does and we both turn toward it, finding him nodding and smiling with a wild look in his eyes as the woman in an older couple pats his face. They leave him and we take up their post.

"Hi there. Getting hit on already, huh?" I ask, accepting his almost desperate hug when he sees me.

"Thank God. I have already made small talk with four couples. *Four*, Janie, and they don't even remember my name. Did they not do their homework about the great Gruff family tree before coming?" He feigns shock.

"Truly irresponsible."

He holds out a hand to Colin, who accepts. I like that Chip doesn't hesitate to welcome him. And this is exactly why we'll tell him the truth.

"So listen, I need to tell you something really quick. And I need you to keep it together and not make a thing of it." I glance at Colin, who dips his chin.

"Um, rude, but okay," Chip says, but he's smiling and waiting for me to get to it.

So I do. "Five years ago, Colin and I got married in Vegas. We did all the paperwork to get it dissolved because..." I shake my head because we don't need to get into all that. "But it turns out the paperwork never went through and it was never finalized. So we're still married."

Chip's eyes flare and he cracks a smile. Still listening.

"Obviously enough, I *do not* want Mom and Dad knowing we're married." My eyes flick to Colin, whose face is unreadable.

"Sure, sure. And there is so much here. But first, I'd like to ask why you haven't subsequently gotten a divorce once you realized it didn't happen years ago, and second, why on earth you would bring this poor man here." He gives Colin a pitying look.

I deeply appreciate that my brother doesn't want to be here any more than I do, though it makes me a little sad, too.

"Well, Colin's in the Army, as you know, and he's getting his next security clearance. That's actually how we found out. And it'll look pretty darn sketchy if it seems like he's been hiding a marriage, or didn't even know he was still married, or really anything like that, so we decided we'd act married for the sake of his work."

Chip is nodding along like this is all perfectly comprehensible to him, the cherub.

"That's lovely. But"—he looks at Colin and presses a hand to his own chest over his heart in apology—"what do you get out of this?"

Leave it to Chip to get right to it. I step closer, lower my voice more, and explain. "We're here together tonight to deter *Barron Banks*." I practically mouth the words, not wanting anyone to overhear the name despite no one being nearby that I can tell.

Chip grins. "Well played. Glad you get something for you. And hey, congrats. Sorry I didn't get to enjoy having a brother for longer than about two minutes."

He holds up his cocktail glass and Colin, now stone-faced, touches his to it right as someone yells for my brother. Chip makes his apologies to us, promises he won't say a word, and then he's gone.

I'm just about to breathe a giant sigh of relief, because that went even better than I'd hoped, when I hear them.

There's this particular way my mother walks in heels on this floor. It's piercing, for lack of a better way to describe it.

There could be fifty other people walking around this house and I would know *her* steps every time.

I catch Colin's eye, his face still a mask of unreadable neutrality, and loop my arm in his. Pulling in a steadying breath, I paste a smile on and chant *you can do this* in my head as we turn.

"Mother. Father. Lovely party."

CHAPTER THIRTY-FIVE

Colin

The Gruffs are just as I remember. They're frozen in time in my memory, always wearing something close to this—a black cocktail dress for her and a dark suit for him. He's aging well though his hair is fully gray and he's smaller than I remember. That's likely a matter of perspective since I was still a boy the last time I saw him.

Mrs. Gruff is tall like Janie. Her hair is still a deep brown color, stylishly curled and swept up in a way that's feminine and effortless. It's clear Janie's her daughter, though the hardness in the set of her mother's jaw is so different from any expression Janie has ever made.

There's a small part of me I buried deep a long time ago that withers in their presence. It's the same part that feels like a boy standing here with their daughter instead of a man who has every right to be here.

But do I? I'll admit the explanation to Chip was painful.

I don't want to rehash the way this is all fake. Real, but fake. I don't want to blame it all on my security clearance and on convincing some silver spoon-fed man-boy he needs to listen to Janie when she says no.

I want, more than I ever have, which is saying something, for this to be real. I want that ring on her left ring finger. I want our cats to live at the same address indefinitely.

"Janie. And who's this?"

Her mother peers at me like she's never seen me. It's certainly possible she doesn't recognize me.

"Mother, Father. You remember Colin Vicente?"

Recognition hits Mrs. Gruff first and her lashes flutter while Mr. Gruff's face screws up in a perplexed frown—at least I think, because his forehead doesn't actually move.

"Well, young man. Hello." This from Mr. Gruff, who extends a hand. "You went to the military academy, didn't you?"

I accept it, shaking slowly. A handshake is more than he ever deigned to offer me before, so that's something. "Yes, sir. I did."

"And?" Mrs. Gruff's tone is replete with an irritation that betrays her belief she's entitled to the details of my life and should be given them without asking.

Janie jumps in before I can. "He's a major in the Army. He's been stationed overseas for years and just moved back to the area."

There's no hint of nervousness in her voice, and the way she clutches my arm makes it almost feel like she's hugging me.

"Whereabouts in the area?" Mr. Gruff asks.

I tell them the unit where I'm now assigned though I don't expect them to know anything about it. Most civilians have only a vague concept about how the military works, usually based on a cousin or uncle or brother's experience. Beyond that, they don't know much and certainly can't identify a specific unit other than the famous ones like the 101st or the 82nd Airborne.

"Of course. And have you met Caldwell Banks? He's contracted on the build-out for the second building they're adding to the small base there." Mr. Gruff pulls out a phone and checks something on the screen, apparently only able to keep his full attention on his daughter and me for a few minutes at a time.

But more surprising is that he clearly does know the building and someone related to Barron Banks is involved there. *Great.*

"I haven't met him, but I've only had a few weeks so far. I moved back about a month ago." Nor would I typically interact with building contractors or project managers or whatever it is Banks does there.

Mr. Gruff hums in a grumbly, unimpressed way. Mrs. Gruff, who has been quiet while her husband led the conversation, turns to Janie.

"How is your work? You're not taking too much time off, are you?" Her tone has an oddly disappointed air to it.

"I'm taking off a little time, but no more than planned."

Janie smiles, but it's thin. Far from the light, beautiful thing I get to see so often.

"And why is it you've brought him?" Mrs. Gruff asks.

Janie barely contains a scoff, but I can see her body jolt. "Because he's my dear friend and also happens to be my boyfriend."

Mrs. Gruff's face falls into a perfect mask and her eyes, vaguely sharklike, shift to target me. "*Him?*"

"Yes, Mother. Him. You know I always—"

"And how is your family, then? Is your father still..." She circles her hand in an odd gesture. *"You know."*

I've had about enough of this. This woman has insulted her daughter and me, and now she's trying to drag out my family's dirty laundry. But I half expected this and now I'm going to make it clear this isn't going to work.

"Actually, yes. We haven't had contact with him in years. My sisters are both well, both thriving. I have three nieces. And my mom is enjoying life. She's an amazing woman."

Janie threads her fingers with mine. "Thanks for having us. Merry Christmas."

She pulls me along with her but I don't need the incentive. I'm happy to leave the Gruffs behind and follow her.

There have been times I've reflected on her upbringing and recognized how much I had in comparison, but for a lot of years, especially high school and the first few years of college, I'd seen it the other way around. I had a deadbeat thief of a father in jail, and we'd scraped by financially once that happened.

Janie's life had seemed so clean. Privileged. *Perfect.*

This small glimpse has given me clarity. I didn't see it as much before, and of course over the years I've made guesses, but one iteration with these people where I didn't feel like the gum on the bottom of their bespoke leather loafers and I get it.

I was the one with the privilege. Janie had money but with it came judgment and expectations and a lot of ugliness. It's genuinely a wonder she and Chip are even halfway decent human beings, let alone the absolutely glorious wonder of a person she is.

She finds a spot next to a smaller but no less fragrant

and beautiful Christmas tree and pulls me into her arms for a hug.

"I'm sorry. I knew they wouldn't be nice but I'd hoped they wouldn't be quite so awful."

I savor her touch and breathe in her scent. Here she is worrying about me when all she got from her parents was criticism veiled as concern.

"I'm fine. I promise." We pull back and she shakes her head, but I stop her by lightly pinching her chin and holding her in place. "Are you okay?"

Her eyes glint, but she nods. "I am. I..."

"You need to come talk to your cousin-in-law?" Andy loops her arm through Janie's and grins at me, then winks. "Can I steal her for just a minute?"

"Of course." Janie could use a dose of Andy's sunshine and she'll be glad to see her cousin, too. "I'll get us fresh drinks."

Janie gives me a look as though searching for whether I'm okay by myself.

"Go ahead. I'll join you in a minute." I lean in to kiss her cheek, resisting the urge to take her mouth instead. As satisfying as it'd be, it's not the time or place.

I watch them go, Andy chattering and gesturing wildly the second they step away, and can't help but smile. I'm glad she has Andy in her life.

Oddly, I'm glad *I* have Andy. I don't know her all that well, but she was instrumental in helping me arrange the cat adoptions and the joy she finds in her business and helping people find their pet is delightful.

Will Gruff approaches, and I instantly stand a bit straighter. The man is taller than me but he's also got this air that says one wrong move may end in a world of hurt. He's not exactly dangerous like some guys I've met, but he's got this sensibility, especially regarding Janie, that tells me he might actually disappear me should I give him a reason, even if he does have a ball of sunshine in human form for a wife.

"Colin." He extends a hand to me.

"Will. Good to see you again." The embarrassed teen in me wants to make an excuse or give a reason why I'm here, but he already knows, and that kid can relax.

"Did you have a nice Christmas? Cats doing well?"

We finish a brief shake and I'm grateful he's given me a clear prompt for conversation.

"We did. And the boys are great. We had a brief moment where we thought one of them had swallowed some ribbon from a package someone dropped off, but it turned out to be a false alarm." The ten minutes yesterday could've been a huge issue, but fortunately we were wrong. Snickerdoodle had batted around part of a bow that had detached from its package and Goob had sat on it.

Janie's cat-proofing had never made more sense than that moment.

Will's chuckling in a knowing way. "You're lucky. We had a cat eat tinsel, and yes, we know very well not to have tinsel with cats. My mother also tried to gift us a poinsettia."

He gives me a wide-eyed look and I've never been more grateful for the time I spent searching the internet for all the things I needed to know about having cats at Christmas. "Yikes."

He nods. "The Honorable Judge Gruff nearly poisoning her grand-cats was rather traumatic for her."

We laugh together for a minute and I'm about to share a story about a guy whose cat ate an entire Christmas garland made of fake pine boughs in my last unit when his subtle smile shifts to something stark enough, my mouth snaps shut.

"Listen. You're a decent man from what I can tell."

I swallow. Nod. Successfully avoid holding my hands together like I'm begging him not to murder me because that's the odd impulse I have.

"Janie is special."

"She is." On this we agree.

He stares at me, inspecting for some hint that will answer his question he hasn't yet asked. But then he nods.

"Good. So let me be clear with you. I'm not a violent man, but you need to treat her with respect. Do right by her. Or we'll have a problem, okay?"

My throat works on a convulsive swallow. "Right. Absolutely, yes. She's—" I won't tell him she's the love of my life, but I can tell him something true. "She's everything."

His gaze narrows for a beat, and then he nods again, clapping me on the back. "Correct."

Without another word, he leaves, working his way back to Andy, who's chatting with someone across the room and smiling. I can't help but join her as I feel Will's approval settle in. I didn't realize I needed it, but I am happy to have it.

"Well, I've got to say, you've got an expert scam going on here."

I turn to find Barron Banks swirling a highball of dark liquid, smirking like he's paid to.

"Scam?" I nod at a waiter and he gives me a "one moment" as he refills his tray.

"Yeah. The one where you're grifting the government with your fake marriage and lying to Janie's family about it?"

There's no more jocular tone or false smile. It's all accusation.

That's when I give him my full attention.

CHAPTER THIRTY-SIX

Colin

Barron Banks sneers before I even speak.

"Don't even try to pretend you don't know what I'm talking about. I heard you earlier with Chip." He takes a drink.

The shot of worry racing through me settles a touch. If he heard us with Chip, then he knows we got married in Vegas—or at least that we didn't realize we've been married all this time.

"The marriage is real—it's legally binding and has been for years at this point." It's not a scam, so his accusation is baseless.

But he leans in, the bourbon on his breath unmistakable and strong. "Sure. But do you think the military will smile on you when they find out you didn't know it was? Do you think your superiors will feel good about a guy who's been pretending he knew all along and is actually a big fake?"

I don't speak. I'm not going to dignify him with a response, but I also don't know how he would have any say in what happens with my military career.

He smirks in a slimy way. "You think you've got her, don't you? But Janie's going to be mine. I'll be here once your fake little marriage implodes right along with your career. And do you know how I know that's going to happen?"

Maybe I'm not as immune to this idiot as I'd like to be because I grit out a, "How?"

He snorts, all triumph. "My dad works where you work—yeah, heard that little tidbit when you were talking to the Gruffs. He'll let slip to a buddy that maybe you aren't what you seem. They'll do some digging." He shrugs a shoulder. "Maybe you lose your security clearance or maybe you get fired outright—no idea. Don't care. Because whatever it is, you'll get sent packing, and Janie won't follow. She's a DC girl and she's not going to follow some deadbeat to a base in Nebraska or Tennessee or Texas. You'll leave. She'll stay." He leans in so close I can feel his breath on my cheek. "I'll win."

Jaw clenched, I breathe through the desire to whirl on this guy and throat-punch him. Just a quick little jab would shut him up and make it tricky to drink his bourbon for a day or two.

But the bigger problem is, he might be right. I don't know how well-connected his father is, but if the military catches wind of this mess, it could be bad. That's where the idea for working with Janie to look like we've always been happily married came from—I wanted to appear above reproach. That's a high bar for anyone, but it *is* the standard for officers and people who have access to top-secret clearances.

As a man whose father was the opposite of above reproach, I hate that I've ended up in a situation to be manipulated by someone like Barron Banks.

I look up to see Janie rushing over to me, worry etched in the lines of her brow. "Are you okay? What was that?"

Clearly, she saw Barron's little whisper session with me.

"He overheard us talking with Chip, and then your parents. He said he's planning to report me via his father and try to get me fired." I finally meet her eyes. "He has big plans for me to get fired and move away and then he'll move in on you."

She doesn't merely scoff. No, this beautiful woman nearly chokes on her reaction to that news. "He's honestly delusional, right?"

There's no point in disagreeing. "He may be. But if his dad is wrapped up in the project over there, he may have connections. I don't know." I give in to the habit of running my hand through my hair.

She sets a hand on my arm. "I'm so sorry. He's a jerk. But we can figure this out, right?"

The smile I offer her is a weak one, but it's not because I'm hopeless or planning to give up. I'm also not about to lose her to Barron Banks. I know there's zero chance that'll happen. I don't have a guarantee Janie and I will work out, but there's no part of me that thinks she'd rather be with him.

And in this odd circumstance, that's growth. I would've looked at a guy like him in a thousand-dollar suit and Italian shoes with a hundred-dollar haircut drinking top-shelf bourbon and thought he was better than me. I did it anytime I saw the cars lining the streets for a party right here in the hallowed halls of Gruff manor.

The people who drove these cars had money. Their

parents were rich and often still married. Their dads were most likely not sitting in prison for bankrupting a veterans' organization.

"Hey, you're not going to lose your career over this. He doesn't know what he's saying."

She's willing me to believe her and to confirm she's right.

But there's a reason I didn't believe my security interview would survive the news that I had no idea I was still married and it's still a concern. Realistically, this could genuinely hurt me.

With that said, I have more clarity now than ever before.

I'm going to go straight to my command team and tell them the truth. I've never liked the lies and I still don't. I don't want them to hear the truth from some jerk whose son is trying to leverage my failure for his gain. I don't want to be the kind of person who's doing something questionable or getting away with something.

I want to be a person of integrity, and I've let myself down on this. Even if it all started in a place of love and fun and yes, stupid impulse, it's spun out into a mess.

So it's time to clean up said mess. And that'll tell me whether I can have what else I want. Because I've worked hard to build a life I'm proud of and a career that someone—no, that Janie—could be proud of.

Being in this fancy house full of people I used to envy hasn't given me satisfaction. It's left me a little empty. None of it is real. What Janie and I could have is the most real thing I've ever imagined and what I've always dreamed of. And I have this wild thought that says I'm already enough, and I probably always was for her. Her family didn't determine my value, nor did my father's actions. My choices have steered my path, yes, but it's what I do now, how I show the kind of man I am professionally and with her, that tells the whole story.

So I'll do what I have to and make this right, and then maybe... maybe then I'll be worthy of her.

CHAPTER THIRTY-SEVEN

Janie

Colin is quiet on the way home.

I'm trying not to freak out but worry knots in my gut. I don't want to feel like this, but I can't stop it. My parents threw his father's jail time in his face. Barron threw our lies in his face.

And now he's just locked away.

My mind is racing. How can I help this?

If there's one thing I know about Colin Vicente, it's that he cares deeply about his career. I've learned up close and personal how much it means to him, and honestly, I'm so proud of him for it. He's worked hard since he turned eighteen and took off to the military academy with so much bravery and heart it kind of breaks mine when I think about it.

He fought in wars. He's lived in three different countries. He's an incredible man.

Losing this life he's built because we were idiots hopped up on tequila and champagne and his mom thought she was doing us a favor just isn't right. None of what we did puts anyone at risk.

By the time we get home and the kitties greet us, I've made a decision. He's still quiet and I have to break through. I have to get us to the place where we can discuss this.

"Will you talk to me?" My voice sounds small in this quiet house.

He shucks his jacket and sighs heavily, but nods. "Of course."

We sit down on the couch, not even taking the time to change out of our party clothes.

"What are you thinking?" I need a hint. Some kind of clue as to where his brain is.

He runs a hand over Goob, who has begun an inspection of us where we sit. "I'm frustrated because I don't like lying. And this whole mess is my fault, as is the lie that is now a problem." His hand cuts through the too-long strands of hair atop his head. "I'm angry that I've put myself in this position."

My heart aches for him. He's not mentioning his father, but I know it's there. "You weren't the only one who had a hand in this. I married you that night of my own free will. I dove in headfirst, too, and I'm sorry I never followed up on the paperwork either. I should've done it just as much as you."

It didn't affect my work in any way, though, and I understand the stakes are lower for me no matter how we slice it.

Unless we think of your heart.

I shove the thought away because I can't be thinking about my heart right now. I'm worried about his.

"Why do you think we did it? Were we really that drunk?"

I huff a frustrated laugh. "I don't know. I certainly didn't arrive in Vegas that weekend planning to marry you."

He eyes me. "No? Because I totally thought that after not speaking to you for years, you'd give me the time of day and end up agreeing to get hitched after less than eight hours in my presence."

A smile cracks through and he returns it, then lifts his arm. I accept the offering, leaning into his side and shutting my eyes against the frustration and headache this whole mess has become.

We sit quietly for a time. Goob and Snickerdoodle curl up on the couch next to us. I want to soak in the peace of this moment and inhale his scent. But I also know what I have to do.

I sit up and take his hands in mine. "We should get the divorce finalized. Then it's just done and we don't—"

"No. No." He's shaking his head, adamant.

"Why not?"

Why oh why is my heart racing? Why does it feel like *right now* is the time for him to say because he doesn't want to. Because he wants to stick with me, to choose me, and he doesn't care what happens otherwise.

His jaw ticks and there's a beat before he says, "It'll look worse that way."

My heart sinks, but I nod. "Ah. Yeah. I'm sure you're right."

I don't want to feel tired and dejected, but I do. It's not fair to him after all the drama tonight, but I just want to crawl in bed, maybe cry a little, and wake up with a fresh mindset and perspective.

"Let's go to bed, okay? We'll figure this out in the morning."

He's frozen, completely inside his head, until he stands and helps me to do the same. But instead of walking back to the bedroom, he moves to collect his jacket.

"What are you doing?"

He swallows, his face so serious and stern. It's an expression I haven't seen in weeks.

"I need to get home and do some work. Compile the timeline of everything. If I'm going to do this, I'm going to do it all the way."

I nod. What else can I do?

I want to tell him he'll manage that more easily after a good night's sleep, but I can see by the set of his jaw and the way his brows are pinched, he won't be sleeping tonight no matter what.

He has to do this, and though it feels like another little prick of our bubble, I get it. I don't blame him at all.

I just wish it didn't hurt so much.

He paces to me and takes my shoulders in his hands. "I want to be clear that I'm going home so I can solve this problem. Get back on track, or face the consequences. I am not running from you. I'm not going to disappear, okay?"

That prompts a watery chuckle from me. "I appreciate that. And I believe you."

When he leaves a few minutes later, after touching his forehead to Goob's and giving Snickerdoodle a rough pet, and of course kissing me so achingly softly it makes me want to cry, he's gone.

I heard what he said and I am going to cling to his

words. He's told me he's not running, he's not disappearing. He's going to deal with the problem.

I believe all of that.

My main concern is that if things don't go well—if he loses his job?

There's a real possibility he'll be reassigned and forced to move. Or maybe he'll have to reinvent himself and find another career, which I suspect will take all of his energy and focus.

I'm not proud of the self-centered thought, but it comes wild and unruly and demanding: *then what about me?*

Janie

Colin texts the next day to say he's been able to set up a meeting with his command team for the day after. I'm honestly impressed because I figured everyone would be on leave, but maybe he's managed it.

He cancels our plans to go to his mom's house for lunch and belated present opening. He reassures me he's working through getting all the evidence to be as upfront as possible and he'll check in with me after the meeting tomorrow.

I try my very best not to feel hurt that he won't come do that work with me. I try and try and try and convince myself I'm succeeding until the doorbell rings and my heart absolutely leaps across the house.

I'm so relieved and convinced it must be him that I swing open the door without checking the spy hole.

My mother stands there waiting for me, her wool coat

black and leather-gloved hands clasped in front of her body like she's here to deliver bad news.

"Mom. Uh, come in."

I step back, wishing for a fleeting moment I had showered and done my hair, then promptly kicking that thought to the curb behind them because I'm in my own home after a long night and I'm not at work. I have every right to have messy hair and sweatpants on.

"Oh. Cats." My mother's tone is clearly disapproving.

"Colin's Christmas present to both of us." I beam because these little beasts have already made me so happy. And so has Colin.

My mother hums disapprovingly, but that's no surprise. She removes her gloves, and I watch her take in the kitchen, nudging a pile of mail I brought in earlier and sniffing when she sees my dirty breakfast dishes in the sink. She's been here one other time right after I moved in and hosted a housewarming party, mostly for my friends. Of course she and my dad stopped by, though begrudgingly.

Now, as it was then, the house is by no stretch of the imagination a mess. Just days ago, we had a photo shoot and it was in virtually pristine condition. Colin and I haven't destroyed it, and yet my mother is walking around like she's inspecting a prison cell.

"Is he here?" Her gaze casts around in search of Colin.

"No. He had some work to do."

"Good." She sits at the corner seat at my dining table. "You shouldn't be with him."

I blink, at first interpreting that to mean I should let him be while he works—that I don't need to hover over him while he attempts to do his man's work. But then it clicks.

An eerie calm comes over me because I realize the only

thing that could've brought her here is precisely what she's just said.

"Why not?"

"You belong with someone else."

"Barron? Is that who you have in mind?" I know it is, so I don't even need to ask, but I want to force her to spell it out.

"Sure. Barron. Or Eaton Chambers. Or Christoffer Walton. Or—"

"So any one of your rich friends' sons?" It's so cliché, it's laughable.

But she's not laughing. "Frankly, yes. It's not about the money, but it *is* about being of a certain... upbringing."

"I grew up with Colin. I've known him practically my whole life. I know his mom and sisters and I just met his brother-in-law and his nieces. I *know* him."

She turns away from me, gaze cast across the room signaling she doesn't care for my response. *Great.*

"Your life is..." She tsks. "It's not what we planned."

This would've been a blow at another time, but in the last few weeks, I've gained perspective. I love my business and I need to continue building it and stop taking what my parents view as handouts via their friends who don't actually want to work with me. I love my friends and my house and now, my cats. Goob isn't mine, but he's Colin's. He's my husband's cat.

And yes, I love my husband. And I'd like to stay married to him if he wants that, too. If whatever happens with his work doesn't destroy our chances.

"I love my life. I'm sorry you don't, but ultimately, it's *my* life."

She turns slowly. "Don't you think it's time to finish up

this little business you've cobbled together and think about doing something with everything you've been given?"

When I don't instantly agree, she continues. "You have so much to offer someone. You could be a real asset to the right man."

"The right—" I don't finish repeating her because I recall she hates this, and I also don't know what I can possibly say to make sense of her. "You want me to give up my business, which is doing well by the way, and find a man."

It's not even a question because now that I've said it, I know that's what she means.

She's been hinting at it for years, growing more and more impatient now that I've reached my thirties like I might expire on the shelf any minute.

"If you're going to fool yourself into thinking you'll make it without a partner, I hate to break it to you, but you're not meant to be alone. You've always needed someone to tow you along beside them, and it might as well be someone powerful and capable who can open doors for you."

It's funny how we've skirted this conversation for years and now that we're having it, I'm not even numb. I'm simply disinterested. And when I realize I have the perfect response, I can't help but lob it her way.

"Well, good news, Mother. I'm already married. To Colin."

Her face falls and her eyes widen. "Since when?"

"A little over five years ago, actually."

Her mouth drops open at this. "Ludicrous! He hasn't even been here. You told us last night he'd just moved back. What kind of marriage is that? You'll divorce him and find someone else. Someone better."

I laugh because there's no other way to handle her right now. "Find someone better? There is no one better. Colin is the best man I know and I've loved him my entire life. Who better can I possibly find? And don't say Barron Banks or another one of the man-children your friends have raised."

I move toward the door and gesture to the exit. "Thanks for stopping by, but I don't think we have anything left to talk about. I'm sorry you don't see value in the choices I've made, but if we're ever going to have a relationship, we're going to have to agree to let one another live their own lives. I hope you'll consider that."

Her nostrils flare slightly and I can see fury and hurt written on her face. There's simply nothing left to say for now. I can't apologize any more for not wanting the life she envisions for me, and any apologies she'd give now would ring false.

She leaves without a word and I sink against the door when I shut it. Snickerdoodle trots over to check on me and I let a few tears slip out. I'm not destroyed but I'm sad. I wish they understood. I wish they could love me for simply being their daughter and not what I achieve or who I marry.

My phone buzzes with a text from Colin, and despite the heavy encounter, my heart flips when I read his message.

"Whatever happens tomorrow, I want to see you after my meeting. Is that okay?"

Silly man. Doesn't he know I'll want him no matter what? Does he think my approval is contingent on a certain outcome tomorrow?

Or is that his way of saying he's going to let me know whether we have a future based off what happens?

There's a nervous trill all through my system and I loose a gusty breath, then get to work. I'm determined not to let assumptions or stubbornness get in the way of what we can have, and since I know he's still working on his master plan, I'm going to do what I can.

I send him dinner courtesy of my favorite delivery app, then dessert, and finally, a photo of me and the boys with a small note. "We love you no matter what."

I press send and every cell in my body wants to burst with nerves and anticipation. Maybe it's too bold.

But maybe he's been telling me all along that he's not running and he just needs to know I'm not, either.

CHAPTER THIRTY-NINE

Colin

Colonel Gleeson has maintained a stern expression throughout the meeting, but he hasn't been unreasonably harsh. He's heard me out and it's honestly more than I've hoped for. Or at least it's more than I've imagined in the darkest times over the last few days.

Reality is, I haven't technically done anything wrong other than make a handful of people believe that my marriage was purposeful and ongoing rather than essentially accidental. He's summed it up in so many words and I get the point.

"I lied, sir, and I'm sorry. I got so focused on my future, on the promotion and clearance for starting this job, and I lost sight of what's most important to me."

He nods, his bald head perfectly smooth, face perfectly shaved. He likely sacrificed his leave beard to be here, and I feel another twinge of guilt burrow in.

"You did lie, technically. I'm not going to excuse that. But I don't believe anything you've told me should disqualify you from working here or from obtaining your clearance."

Relief rushes through me so quickly I'm lightheaded. "Thank you" isn't the right thing to say here, but before I can figure out what is, he continues.

"That said, it's not going to purely rest with me. Yes, I'm in command here and I could probably make the call. But this is a unique enough circumstance, especially if someone like Banks Industries is involved, I want you to be cleared completely. I'll assemble a board of sorts to review the events, your explanations and evidence, and they'll adjudicate appropriately."

"Understood. If there's anything I can do to help, please say the word, sir."

He stands, so I rise, too, and accept the hand he offers.

"You're a good man, Colin. I'm sure however the board rules, you'll have learned the lesson here." He's got absolutely crystal-blue eyes and they are lasering into mine like they can hypnotize me into that being the truth.

There's no need, because he's right. "Absolutely, sir. Lesson learned and I'll need no repeats."

"Good man. I'll be in touch about the board, but I'd like to have them meet just after the new year."

I didn't expect him to call more people in during a time when most take leave, but a part of me had hoped this would all be resolved sooner. Still, I thank him again and exit his office.

My pace increases as I step outside the building into the bitterly cold December air. It almost feels like it could snow, and I'm eager to get home.

Eager to get back to Janie and our two cats. The photo she sent of her with the boys just about burned away all my resolve to stay at my place and focus. I'd printed out every shred of evidence I had—plane tickets to Vegas, receipts from the chapel that night and a paper trail with the lawyer we'd used to address the divorce.

Would I rather have been with Janie? Yes a hundred times. I didn't want to lock myself away, but I also knew that if my career was riding on how I presented myself and the information that would corroborate the fact that I had not realized I was married for a decent reason, I had to focus completely. I didn't want to leave anything to chance or look back and wonder whether I could've done something more.

As I drive to Janie's, I know. I've done everything I could aside from come clean from the get-go and not try to avoid the consequences for not only getting married in Vegas, but not following up.

In another man's story, he might wonder how he neglected to do so. Especially someone who tended to be reliable and responsible—who appreciated honesty and valued his integrity.

But my story centered around Janie. My answer here did, too.

I didn't look to see if we were divorced because I couldn't stand to think about how we'd gotten married—that we'd done it in the throes of a foolish night and yet it was the thing I'd always wanted. I couldn't bear the thought of seeing her signature on paperwork that would put an end to the marriage, as unanticipated as it had been.

Her name there would've been so final, a line in the sand that ultimately couldn't be erased. So I didn't look so I wouldn't see the end.

On this side of it all, I had more clarity than I'd ever dreamed. Yes, I valued my job. It'd given me purpose when I had none, focus when I lacked it, and a way forward when I felt like I was drowning in the shame of my father's choices and the sense that I'd never shake the grime of his embarrassing ways from my clothes.

But it's just that—just a job. A career, yes, and one that matters. But at some point, whether it's in a few weeks or a decade or somewhere in between, I'll end my time as a soldier. I will get out or retire and I'll move into the civilian world. Some people might care about what I did in the military but still more, if we're being honest, will not. They'll smile and nod, maybe mumble a "thank you for your service," and they'll move on.

For me, I'll always carry the honor and scars of this life with me. I will never forget the people we lost on deployments, the families I guided in company command, and the experiences afforded to me the world over. Never. I will be honored if I can continue on here and into the future, but I will not falter or lose myself if the board comes down with a no.

It won't be simple, but it is clear.

I want more from my life than just the military. I want Janie. I want our little buddy cats to live together, not apart. I want to build a family, if she wants that.

"We love you no matter what."

That message fueled me. The photo, the picture, then a few minutes later a knock on my door. I jumped up thinking maybe it was her, but it was food. She sent me food. She took care of me, even when I was putting space between us so I could focus and so maybe she could figure out how she really felt.

But Janie already knew. So often, I hadn't given her the choice. I'd taken it from her by leaving. That's why I made clear I'd be back, that I wasn't running.

But now I am. I'm running back to her and I'm staying as long as she'll have me.

CHAPTER FORTY

Janie

The doorbell rings about an hour after his meeting started and I'm hoping it's him. I've been pacing, the cats eyeing me from their spots on the back of the couch, and when I hear the bell, I race to the front of the house.

I yank the door open to find Colin. He's painfully handsome in his uniform, the same one he wore in Vegas.

"Hi." His smile is bright and loose.

"It must've gone well if you're smiling." I grin, relieved for him, but he's shaking his head.

"I actually don't know yet. The meeting went as well as it could've, but they'll need to convene a board to avoid any appearance of favoritism or bias, especially since Banks Industries may be alerted and that makes it messy."

His gaze rakes over me like he's hungry for the view and despite what sounds like mediocre news, my heart is bursting with happiness to see him again. To know that he came directly here.

"Come in." I step aside, holding the door for him, but he shakes his head.

Then he drops to one knee right there on my front stoop, in his fancy uniform. The hand that had been behind his back swoops out to reveal a stunning bouquet of bright red flowers mixed with greens and winter berries that looks so Christmassy and romantic, I laugh.

"This is fancy." I take the bouquet, laughing and a little breathless because he's so handsome, and this whole kneeling in front of me thing is a lot.

I tilt my head, waiting for him to rise to his feet, but he stays there for one second, two. I'm about to insist he come inside out of the cold when he holds out his hand.

Reflexively, I place mine in his. He holds tight, and then he begins.

"Janie 'Cabbage Patch' Gruff..."

I laugh, then suck in a breath as a realization hits.

"I have loved you since the day I met you, and I have been in love with you since sometime around your thirteenth birthday."

My lashes flutter and I huff out a breath, but I don't speak because he's continuing.

"I have spent far too long running from you for fear you'd break my heart. I was scared I wasn't good enough for you, convinced that my family, or just *me*, wasn't good enough."

I shake my head, but he gives me a look that tells me he knows, he's getting there, so I bite my lip and wait with every last bit of patience I possess.

His warm hand squeezes mine. "Before I say anything else, I need to confess that I didn't drink all that much in

Vegas. Just enough to cut away the layer of those fears and let me see what I wanted, and of course, it was you."

A watery laugh escapes. "I have to admit I was pretty drunk. But I think even if I hadn't been, I would've done the same thing."

His eyes brighten with hope, and I want to tell him he doesn't need to hope, but it's not my turn yet.

"For me, Janie, it's always been you. As angry with my mom as I was when I found out the divorce never went through, there was a big part of me that could feel it was right that way. I know it sounds crazy, but I—"

"I get it. I do." And I genuinely do. As upsetting as it was, it also felt like fate. Or something that had bound us together that wouldn't be severed by accident.

"Good. So, I'm hoping in the context of the time we've spent in the last few weeks and the message you sent last night, you might consider being my wife."

I grin, completely elated, and say, "Of course. I already am."

"You are. But I want you to stay that way. For good. I'm asking if you'll marry me—*stay* married to me. I want you to be mine indefinitely and I want to have kids and build a life and—"

With every bit of strength I have, I pull him to his feet and press my mouth to his. I'm laughing and crying and kissing him. His hands wrap around my back and hold me close, close, close.

"That a yes, CP?"

Another laugh bursts out of me. "Yes, you stubborn, silly man. I love you, too, and of course it's a yes."

The door has been open this whole time and Goob and Snickerdoodle have intrepidly joined us. Colin's brow furrows and then he jumps, reaching down for something I don't see until he pulls Snickerdoodle up off the slacks of his uniform.

"Did he just climb you?" I ask, amused and a little horrified.

"He did. Might be time to trim the nails," he says, holding the cat away from his body so it doesn't snag on the jacket of his uniform.

I quickly gather the little mischievous fluff into my arms. "So relatable, my little friend, and yet we don't want to do that to your dad's uniform."

The smile on Colin's face is so bright, you'd think being father to my cat is the better part of the deal here.

"Come on, Goob. Let's get you boys a treat," I say, and the elderly little cat toddles inside after me and Snickerdoodle. Colin shuts the door behind us and we all move into the kitchen.

"Mind if I change?" He's unbuttoning the jacket of his uniform.

The action makes me realize I never got to do that. Not after our wedding in Vegas, and not ever since. We've been married in more than name only, of course, because we've been supporting each other and navigating so much. But we haven't gotten to enjoy each other like a married couple should.

"Janie? That okay?"

I nod instantly, shoved from the trance I entered as he slipped each brass button through its buttonhole.

"Yes, sorry." I set Snickerdoodle down and approach, summoning some of the boldness he just showed with all of his honesty. "I was thinking how I should get to do that."

I settle my hands over his at the center button and take over when he lets his arms fall to his sides. His gorgeous eyes hold mine and I work my way down, button by button.

We slip the jacket off and he holds it over his forearm. I go to work on his white shirt.

One button, two. Our gazes don't waver but my breath is growing heavy. Three, four, five... how many buttons are on a shirt, anyway? I help him out of the shirt, and tug at the undershirt tucked into the dark blue trousers.

"Oh, you meant all of it." A smile flashes and his eyes flicker with heat.

I nod. "I meant all of it."

Goob trills a meow and leans up with one paw against my thigh like he's checking in.

"We'll be back, buddy. You hang out here for a bit." Colin pats Goob's head, then laces his fingers through mine and kisses the back of my hand. One more flash of mischief, and he's upended me, carrying me in a bridal hold to my room.

Our room.

Because we are husband and wife, and we're finally embracing it.

"I guess we'll talk more about your meeting later?" I ask, but I'm pressing kisses to the line of his jaw and my hands are wandering.

He chuckles low. "A bit later, yeah."

CHAPTER FORTY-ONE

Colin

As we sit with pizza and glasses of red wine, candles lit and the cats snoozing on the couch, her ring on that left finger and my heart completely in her hands, I could laugh or weep or both with how good it feels to know she's really, truly mine.

There are lingering issues to discuss, though. Even after an afternoon of bliss, it's only now we're circling back around to talk through everything that's ahead.

"So hopefully next week, you'll know the future of your career?" She takes a sip of wine.

"The immediate future, at least. There's never a guarantee in the military and obviously part of why I was so wound up coming here is because I know I'm going to have to work hard to impress my new command team and get the marks I need for promotion to lieutenant colonel. That may be blown anyway, but I can't do anything about it at this point."

She nods, chewing a bite of her pizza. I take a taste of my slice.

"I hate this situation so much, but I'm not mad about where we've ended up." The pretty blush on her cheeks deepens and she reaches out to grasp my hand.

"Me, too." I clear my throat, forcing the nerves to calm so I can get this part out. "And I know we've just essentially said we're in this for real now, but there are some aspects to our lives we need to think through."

"I told you I'll move. I wasn't joking about that."

I'm already shaking my head. "That's nonsense, though, Janie. You have such a full life here and your business is already a success, never mind what's about to happen when that article comes out and everyone who reads it wants to work with you. It may not even be an issue if I can't continue in military life, but if things go the way I hope, I *will* leave DC. It's so unlikely I could stay here for the rest of my career, and frankly, I wouldn't want to. But that's if I'm only thinking about myself. So I want to tell you that I'll do my best on that. And we'll—"

"Can you listen to my reasoning for a minute? I think you'll understand what I'm saying if you do."

She's so calm and steady, I have no choice but to listen, not that I'd want anything else.

"I'm not ready to leave DC right now. Not this year. I'm still building. But I've been building this business in one way or another for almost a decade now. I've been in DC for my entire life, save some travel and my time in Boston. I think moving around a little could be an adventure."

After a giant exhale, I try not to burst her bubble. "It can be. But there are also places that are kind of the worst for one reason or another. And that's not even considering things like schools for kids or—" My gaze shifts from her to my plate because I may have taken this too far.

I hear her chair scrape back from the table and in another few seconds, she's drawing my face toward her, waiting for my eyes to meet hers as she sits in the chair next to me.

"Why'd you stop?"

Nowhere to hide now, and I don't even know why I am. Still breaking bad habits, I guess. "We haven't talked about kids. I didn't want to overwhelm you."

She gives me a full smile before wiping it away and returning to the serious expression she wore before. "I want kids. Especially with you. And from what I've heard friends say, there's no real preparation for it. So we can't know how that'll go for us. Just like we don't know what military life will be like together. Who knows, you might hate having me with you."

"Never."

She grins again. "What I do know is that I've spent far too much of my life away from you and anything I can do to avoid that in the future, I will. It may not always be possible, but I don't love this business more than I love you."

"You shouldn't have to choose, though. That's not fair."

"And you?" Her palms cup my cheeks. "How much have you had to give up?"

I can't accept this notion, though. "That doesn't matter. I made this choice from the beginning. Now I'm asking you to rearrange your whole life to accommodate *my* career."

The soft smile she gives me fills me up despite the mix of worry and frustration.

"I appreciate that. I do, honestly. But I need you to believe me when I say I'm not worried. I also know that I will probably have some angst about it when the time comes, but my hope is I'll be able to hand it off to someone here and then maybe I open an expansion, or a travel arm of my business and it can continue growing."

"That'd be amazing. I love that idea." I brush her hair behind one ear.

"Me, too. See? We've already figured it out."

She grins, and I haul her to me and bury my face in her neck while we hug.

We pull back and she presses a soft kiss to my lips, then skitters around to her seat and takes a giant bite of pizza. I do the same and once we're talking again, she admits, "I don't know how it'll go. But I do know we've had plenty of time apart. We've both been able to build careers and travel. I don't want that to come to a screeching halt, but I'm ready for a new phase. Maybe some of that will be expanding that business." She shrugs one shoulder. "Maybe it'll be on maternity leave. Who knows?"

This woman. She knows exactly how to charm me, though I'm an easy mark for her.

"I love you. So much." I've said it a dozen times today and I'm not sure when it'll slow down.

"I love you, too."

Her beaming smile is fuel to the fire that hasn't stopped burning between us, and soon, our pizza and wine are abandoned for better pursuits.

That night as we settle into bed, she snuggles into my side while we both read.

"Hey, what are we doing for New Year's Eve?"

The pads of my fingers trace a figure eight on her arm. "Whatever you want."

She rests her head against my shoulder. "Just promise

me you'll kiss me at midnight. I used to dream you'd show up at one of my parents' parties and—" She sighs.

I sit up and she does, too.

"What?"

"Are you telling me you wanted me to come kiss you at midnight when we were younger? Like teen years?"

Her eyes skate around like she's not sure why I'm being weird. "Yes?"

I laugh. "I cannot tell you how many years I talked myself out of doing just that. The last year I lived at home, I even walked over to your house."

"You did? Are you kidding me? Why didn't you come in?" Her face is borderline devastated, and even more so when she sees my expression shift.

My cheeks heat and then she's moving, up and straddling me, hands on my shoulders, bright eyes intense on mine.

"You didn't come in because of them, right?"

I nod. I don't like thinking back to how small I felt standing outside their palatial house longing to go inside and find her, kiss her, finally tell her how I felt, but knowing absolutely nothing could come of it.

"Did I tell you my mom stopped by yesterday? Tried to convince me to scrap my business and get married like a nice little girl?"

I growl for what must be the first time in my life, but she grins and steals a kiss.

"Exactly. And then when I told her I had gotten married five years ago to you and we were still married, she was *not* happy."

A chuckle stumbles out of me because she's telling this story with so much animation, I can't help it. But the beauty here is, it's not making me doubt that we belong together. I can't doubt that anymore because regardless of what her parents think or what my father did, we've *chosen* each other. More than once, by now.

"I told her I've loved you all my life and there's no one else for me. That's true." Her eyes shimmer and I grip her at her waist, savoring the connection between us. "I hate that we missed so many years, but I don't want to dwell there. I want to look forward."

"Me, too."

She grins. "Good. And promise me you'll always kiss me at midnight, as long as we're together."

"I promise."

EPILOGUE

Janie

In what I'm learning is true military style, what ideally would've been a few days' wait turned into four weeks of uncertainty. But when Colin shows up at my office with a gorgeous bouquet and a huge grin, I know the result.

"Still a soldier?" I ask as he hugs me and swings me around.

He stops, groans in mock agitation. "Hey, once a soldier, always a soldier."

"Oh, right. Sorry. I've got to learn this stuff."

"That's right, you do, Mrs. Vicente." He grimaces. "Okay, hated that."

I tsk. "Me, too. I think I'll stick with Janie Gruff."

He laughs and kisses me, at first a quick happy peck, then deeper. It's only the knock on the clear wall that has us pulling apart.

"Guess maybe we should save that for later." He winks like he's got plans.

Little does he know.

I've got plans, too. We'll be starting a family a lot sooner than either of us anticipated, and though I was shocked initially, it clicks into place. It fits. And I'm so happy to be building our family already. But Goob and Snickerdoodle are going to help me break that news, and for now, we're going to focus on his victory.

"But listen, I know we've talked about this. I just want to say one more time that if this isn't what you want, you matter more to me and I will drop my packet *today* if you think this isn't right for us. I'll figure out something else and we can stay here forever and—"

"Thank you, Colin. Truly. But I'm here for whatever comes our way while you're in the Army, and long after it, too."

His smile is a sunrise. "You're just too good, CP."

I laugh. "Nah, but I'm yours."

"Thank God." He huffs a laugh, and I join him, but then he adds, "And I'm yours. Always have been."

Thank you for reading Married Christmas, Happy Holidays! I hope you loved Janie and Colin (and Goob and Snickerdoodle). If you haven't yet, check out the first two books in the Married to the Military Series! They're also marriage of convenience Christmas romcoms. You'll get to see Grace and Justin's story in I'll Be Married for Christmas and Andy and Will Gruff's story in Have Yourself a Married Little Christmas.

And if you've already enjoyed those, why not check out a little story set at a German Christmas market and see what Colin and his mom might've seen when she visited him? You can find that story in Waiting on Love at Christmas.

AUTHOR'S NOTE AND ACKNOWLEDGMENTS

These two were tricky. They had so much baggage that I found making them lighthearted a challenge. Honestly, I love nothing more than some angst and an "It's always been you" scenario, which you've no doubt noticed if you've read a handful of my books. So I think this one had a little less "com" in the romcom, and I decided to be okay with that. This was their story as it needed to be told. I ended up absolutely loving them, and I hope you did too!

Huge thanks to my beta readers Amanda and Genny, and a special thanks to Genny for challenging me to push into the THEN a bit more than I had planned. I love the way that turned out—as usual, you were right!

Thank you so much to Zee Monodee for editing and to Theresa Schultz of Marginalia Editing for the proof! Any errors persisting here are, as always this imperfect human person's right here (insert me, Claire Cain).

Thank you to everyone who continues to take a chance on my books, and a huge thanks to Jess Mastorakos for the covers that make people want to!

Thank you, readers, for being here. I hope it gave your Christmassy, holiday feelings and got you in the spirit to celebrate (or sit on the couch and be cozy with your cat). I hope you know in your head and heart how miraculous and beloved you are!

(Oh, and to the *NSYNC Christmas Album... thanks for all the good times, past, present, and future.)

ABOUT THE AUTHOR

Claire Cain lives to eat and drink her way around the globe with her traveling soldier and three kids, but is perhaps even happier hunkered down at home in a pair of sweatpants and slippers using any free moment she has to read and cook. Or talk—she really likes to talk. She has become an expert at packing too many dishes in too few cabinets and making houses into homes from Utah to Germany and many places in between. She's a proud Army wife and is frankly just really happy to be here.

You can also join Claire's facebook reader group for exclusive content and fun: https://www.facebook.com/groups/clairecain/

Website: http://www.clairecainwriter.com

E-mail: Claire@ClaireCainWriter.com

Newsletter sign-up for new releases, exclusives, and freebies, including a free book:

http://www.clairecainwriter.com/newsletter

amazon.com/author/clairecain

bookbub.com/authors/claire-cain

instagram.com/clairecainwriter

facebook.com/clairecainwriter

goodreads.com/clairecainwriter

pinterest.com/clairecainwriter

tiktok.com/@clairecainwriter